BE GOOD
BE REAL
BE CRAZY

Also by Chelsey Philpot
Even in Paradise

CHELSEY PHILPOT

BE GOOD
BE REAL
BE CRAZY

HARPER TEEN
An Imprint of HarperCollinsPublishers

For Levi,

I

    fell

        in

            love.

That changes everything.

Lines from the Rumi poem "A Moment of Happiness" used courtesy of the translator, Coleman Barks.

HarperTeen is an imprint of HarperCollins Publishers.

Library of Congress Cataloging-in-Publication Data
Names: Philpot, Chelsey, author.
Title: Be good be real be crazy / Chelsey Philpot.
Description: First edition. | New York : HarperTeen, [2016] | Summary:
"Homer, Mia, and Einstein are three aimless teenagers searching for
meaning on an epic road trip up the East Coast—a journey that will
take them to the most unexpected places"— Provided by publisher.
Identifiers: LCCN 2016000194 | ISBN 9780062293725 (hardback)
Subjects: | CYAC: Automobile travel—Fiction. | Self-realization—
Fiction. | Friendship—Fiction. | BISAC: JUVENILE FICTION
/ Social Issues / Friendship. | JUVENILE FICTION / Family /
Siblings.
Classification: LCC PZ7.P5496 Be 2016 | DDC [Fic]—dc23 LC record
available at http://lccn.loc.gov/2016000194

Typography by Erin Fitzsimmons
16 17 18 19 20   PC/RRDH   10 9 8 7 6 5 4 3 2 1
❖
First Edition

Listen to the scientist . . .

"Do not look at stars as bright spots only. Try to take in the vastness of the universe."

—*Maria Mitchell*

the poet . . .

"In the universe, there are things that are known, and things that are unknown, and in between, there are doors."

—*William Blake*

the philosopher . . .

"All things in the universe arrange themselves to each person anew."

—*Ralph Waldo Emerson*

and then, perhaps, write your own. . . .

THE PARABLE OF
LOPSIDED LOVE

ONCE UPON A TIME, THERE was a gentle giant of a boy and he fell in love with an unknowable mystery of a girl who did not, could not, love him back—at least not in the way he loved her.

When did their one-sided romance begin? The day they first met? Was that when his heart flooded? It was so strange that he could remember everything else about that afternoon and not that one detail.

It was a beautiful Tuesday in June on the small island paradise off the coast of Florida. The Girl didn't drift into La Isla Souvenirs the way that most tourists did, sliding their hands over bric-a-brac, clicking and clacking shot glasses against one another, rubbing the T-shirts between their fingers to gauge the scratchiness of the cheap cotton.

No, she pushed her way between the stuffed racks and packed shelves as if her default mode was to anticipate resistance. Her feet were bare and coated with a layer of white sand. Her hair was the color of fruit punch and her left ear was a semicircle of silver, copper, and plastic piercings.

She didn't say anything as she made her way toward the jewelry display on the wall near the dressing room. She hummed like she wanted to be heard while she picked up tacky necklace after tacky necklace. She tried on all the plastic bangles at once and wiggled her arm in the air, making them rattle like pebbles trapped in a balloon. She slipped cheap rings onto her left hand until all five fingers were hidden and then shook them off, letting each one fall onto the aluminum display tray with a *ping*.

The first time her eyes met his in the warped floor mirror, the Boy blushed and changed the paper in the cash register, even though the roll in there was far from done. The second time, she smiled and puckered her lips like a fish. He laughed. The third time, she crossed her eyes and stuck out her tongue. He laughed again. He laughed all the times after, too.

Her exit was as abrupt as her entrance. She left slapping her feet to an inconsistent rhythm that oddly complemented her off-key humming. When she reached the place where the shade from the store's awning stopped and the sun-baked wood of the boardwalk began, she paused, spun on the balls of her feet, and smiled. Before the Boy thought to smile back, she was gone, leaving her footprints on the floor and a feeling of emptiness where there had been none before.

The Boy knew he should have stopped her. He should have

asked her to turn out her pockets or called his dads to the front or recited the warning on the sign taped to the cash register, the one that promised, "All Shoplifters Will Be Prosecuted to the Fullest Extent of the Law." But he did none of those things.

Maybe he *had* started loving her that first afternoon? When, after all, does the fall begin—at the first thought of flight or the moment you're airborne?

However, the Boy *could* tell you the exact moment he *knew* he loved her. It was 3:03 p.m. on a July Thursday. She had just come through the curtains that separated the front of the store from the back. Her shoulders were hunched, her steps uncertain. On her wrist was the rope bracelet he had seen her take the first day. The Boy liked the idea of sharing a secret with her, so he never told his dads—not before, and certainly not after they hired her.

The curtain was still swinging behind her when the Girl looked up and saw him watching her. "I need your help," she said.

Four.

Very.

Simple.

Words.

In that moment, the universe paused.

In that moment, he felt the bliss of being needed, of having a purpose. In that moment, he *knew* he was in love.

He understood from the beginning that she could not love

him back the same way he loved her. She was too not-of-this-place. Too strangely beautiful to love a confused boy with a worried heart.

Theirs would be a lopsided love. But it would be enough.

It had to be.

THE ISLAND AT THE END OF THE WORLD—OR MAYBE JUST FLORIDA

HOMER ONLY NEEDED TO HEAR the opening chords of the song about to play on La Isla Souvenirs' ancient stereo to know that he had to change the station—and fast. Unfortunately, he didn't even have time to turn around before his brother's voice traveled loud and clear from behind the men's swimsuit rack.

"I love this song. Homes, turn it up."

His eyes still on the computer screen and the order form he'd been working on all morning, Homer reached back and slowly turned the ball of tape that served as the volume knob on the store's stereo until the music faded from mind-numbing to a mere murmur.

"Hey—" Einstein's voice cracked with indignation as a hanger from the swimsuit rack caught the neck of his T-shirt. "Not cool, Homes."

Homer raised both arms above his head like he was stretching.

"Awww." He forced a yawn as he turned around. "Would you believe the sound system's broken again?" Homer dropped his arms and immediately focused his eyes on the computer screen so he wouldn't have to meet Einstein's stare.

"You're the worst liar in the whole world," Einstein said as he shook himself loose. "I hate these new hangers."

Homer glanced down at his little brother. His round cheeks and the fact that he was short for his age made Einstein look younger than thirteen. Add in his puffy afro, smudgy glasses, and rotating selection of cheesy science T-shirts, and it was no wonder strangers talked to him like he was ten. "How can you see through all that gunk? Here." Homer grabbed the roll of paper towels from beside the stereo and tossed it to Einstein. The roll hit the floor and opened like a carpet, stopping when it hit the legs of the beach umbrella display. "Guess they don't teach hand-eye coordination at Mercy State University, huh?"

"Don't change the topic." Einstein grunted dramatically as he bent forward. "D.B. said I get to be in charge of the music the first week of break. Dad, isn't that what you said?" Einstein's voice rose and cracked as he ripped a square of paper from the roll and halfheartedly wiped his glasses.

"Steiner, I'm in the front of the store. Not on another island. No need to shout." The top of D.B.'s head appeared over the shelves nearest the store's entrance, the ones that were stuffed with beer koozies, cheap sunglasses, pinwheels, and plastic plantain figures. The floorboards, swollen with humidity and worn by years and years of shoppers coming and going, creaked under D.B.'s feet as he walked toward the counter. "What is it, my beloved second born?"

Einstein ignored D.B.'s sarcasm. "Homer is messing with the music and it's my choice today."

"I don't know how you can like that song," Homer interrupted. "The lyrics are ridiculous. Listening to it is a betrayal of your species or something."

"First, Apollo Aces is awesome," Einstein sniffed. "And second, what do you mean by my 'species'? The socially inept?"

"No." Homer leaned against the wall, taking care not to crack his head on the shelf behind the cash register. "I mean the genius *sapiens* species. I bet you're the only genius in the world who loves Apollo Aces's mindless pop ballads. What would your idols at I-9 think if they knew?"

Einstein scoffed so hard his glasses, which were somehow even more smudged than before he cleaned them, slid to the ball of his nose. "So now you're maligning my choice of role models as well as my musical preferences?" Einstein crossed his arms. "For the record, I imagine that Dr. Az and the other I-9 scientists are very open-minded when it comes to cultural tastes—unlike *some* individuals."

"Okay," D.B. interrupted. "Homes, just because you're a giant doesn't mean you get to be music dictator. Steiner, you know your father and I fully support your intellectual curiosity."

"Thank you."

"Especially if it should lead to a billion-dollar discovery that allows us to retire while we're still young and extremely handsome." D.B. paused. "That said, you are a certified genius. Can't you come up with a hobby that's a little less morbid than studying the demise of humanity?"

"*Et tu*, D.B.?" Einstein pressed his hands over his heart. "The world's leading physicist says the planet could get sucked into a black hole in a few weeks and you guys are more worried about the glow stick order getting here in time for New Year's Eve than about whether human beings will still be around to celebrate." Einstein flung his hands in the air, nearly knocking over an inflatable palm tree. "Is Mia the only person on this island who understands me?" Einstein waited for the palm tree to stop swaying before he continued. "Mia doesn't think I-9 and Dr. Az are a joke. In fact, she thinks they're both 'super-duper fascinating.'" Einstein raised one eyebrow. "Her words exactly."

Homer coughed and started straightening the rows of Chap-Sticks in the cardboard display next to the cash register. *Of course Mia will listen to Einstein ramble for hours.*

"On that note, Madame Curie is out of mice, so if anyone needs me, I'll be at the pet store," Einstein said. A few stomps later, he was on the boardwalk and out of sight.

"I really hope he grows out of this I-9 thing. The snake thing would be good, too." D.B. sighed, but quickly pasted a smile on his face as he waved at a woman and a little girl in matching green sundresses who were sifting through a bin of tie-dye tank tops. "How's it going, folks. [...] post-Thanksgiving bonanza." He pointed to [...] above the bin. "Fifteen percent off all weekend.

"Hey, Dad," Homer said, tapping the side of the [...] puter screen. "You want to come look at this before I s[...] He made a few adjustments to the spreadsheet and then slid [...] from behind the counter so D.B. could slide in.

"Did you grow overnight? You get taller. Einstein's hair and brain get bigger." D.B. frowned and wiggled the mouse side to side, but when a family of four shuffled past, he smiled. "Hi there, folks. Everything's fifteen percent off." He pointed to the sign again. "Part of the annual end-of-the-year sale."

"Well, isn't that just our luck." The man spoke like he was storing marshmallows in his cheeks.

Homer waited until the dad, mom, daughter, and son were by the shelves in front of the changing rooms before he whispered, "Ten bucks. Suburb of Omaha."

"You're on," D.B. said, turning his eyes back to the computer. "This order looks good. I'll send it this afternoon. The stock should be here for you and Mia to go through on Monday." D.B. whirled around so quickly, Homer was startled into leaning back. "Speaking of Mia," D.B. continued, "I need you to stop by her place on your way home."

"Why?" Homer felt his cheeks prickle.

"I need you to remind her about the lot."

Homer suddenly felt like all the spit had been vacuumed out

...e again? It's not like it's easy

But I've had Doug and his crew

I ask again, I'm not sure the lot will

of his ? tapped his knuckles against the coun-

to¢ times, then looked up at the ceiling—key

out

ᴌ rant was coming on.

ᴌch as that poor kid has had to move around, all

ƀeen through," he said, "it's a freaking miracle that

_____ out so great, so positive." D.B.'s voice got louder. "Mia's story is a damn case study, a freaking perfect example of how messed up the system is. And not just in Alabama." D.B. exhaled. "Mia was born in Alabama, right?"

"I think so."

"Anyway, it's messed up here in Florida, too. Your dad and I were lucky, plain and simple. We had a great attorney. Adopting you and Einstein was just a matter of paperwork and patience."

"Yeah, I know."

When D.B. looked at Homer, his eyes glistened at the corners, but his hands were knotted into fists. "Kids shouldn't be shuffled around like pieces in a board game." His voice softened to just above a whisper. "You'd have to be superhuman to go through all that and not end up with some scars."

"Dad?"

D.B. sighed. "Yes, my one-and-only firstborn?"

"I'll remind her. Can I go now?" Homer asked, already

shuffling toward the back office. "I want to catch Mia before her shift."

"Go on," D.B. replied, the tension in his body melting like a Popsicle on a summer afternoon. "Remind her that she's welcome to stay with us. And that if there's anything we can do, we'll do it." He pressed his hands against the counter. "It takes a village. Really does. And she doesn't have to do it alone."

"I'll tell her."

"Good."

Mia was perched on the deck of her small sailboat, her tan arms folded over the lower railing and her legs swinging against the sides as if the boat was bobbing on gentle waves instead of planted on asphalt. Her hair was pulled back in a loose ponytail that left long strands of cherry red drifting around her face. Her body was turned toward Homer, but she was looking forward over the bow at the harbor.

Most of the time, Homer couldn't help but smile when he saw her. But every now and then, just thinking about Mia caused his insides to feel like hurt and anxiety had declared war and both sides were winning.

It wasn't anything she said or did. It was all the things Mia didn't say or do. She never mentioned La Isla de Plátanos using the future tense or called it her "home." She cheerfully refused to move into an apartment, preferring her house on wheels. And though she hated to wear shoes, she always had a pair with her. If she had kept flip-flops or wedges in her purse, Homer would have thought nothing of it. But she carried sneakers, and sneakers were made for running.

Homer literally tried to shake his thoughts from his head as he moved across the lot. But when he stopped at the circle of junk around the *S.S. Canterbury*, his brain was still buzzing.

Homer and Einstein had helped Mia build her "gate" two days after she started working at the store. The memory of how methodically Einstein had gathered sun-faded beer cans to decorate the entrance posts—two shredded tires—made Homer smile. When Homer had found two buoys on the beach, both stained green with dried sea gunk, Mia had squealed and hugged him around the waist. He'd been amazed and a little stupefied at how easy it was to make her happy. It had been a good day.

"Hey, you." Mia's voice shocked Homer back into the present.

"Oh, hey." Homer stopped a few feet out from the tire posts, just far enough that he had to look up to see her. She was still resting her chin on her arms, swinging her legs, looking at Homer now instead of the water.

"Question. Do you think I look Old McGee-ish today?" Each time one of Mia's heels connected with the hull, a sound, like someone playing a huge drum far in the distance, boomed. *Thump. Thump. Thump.*

"Sorry. What'd you ask?" Homer had to take his hand out of his pocket to shield his eyes as he looked up.

"You know, I'm turning twenty exactly three days after the world's supposed to end. Einstein told me." Mia raised her arms above her head, stretching them behind her and arching her back so that her T-shirt pulled against the round ball of her stomach. "December twenty-third, the date I officially become old."

"How can you listen to Einstein's rambling? It's so depressing."

"I think it's interesting." Mia shrugged. "The Giant Atom Accelerator is a forty-thousand-ton cylinder, eighteen miles beneath the ground in a deserted corner of a vast continent. It's capable of moving subatomic particles at . . . Ugh, I forget the word Einstein uses."

"I'm impressed you can recite that much."

"Oh, wait. I know more." Mia sat up straighter, one hand pressed to her temple as she continued. "Though this experiment is an extraordinary accomplishment for science, Dr. Az, the world's foremost expert on existential risks and founder of the I-9 Institute for the Study of Probable Doom, Existential Risks, and Apocalyptic Possibilities, believes it could be a disaster for humanity. The chance that colliding atoms will cause a giant black hole to open over the Earth is significantly more probable than the chance that the Giant Atom Accelerator will successfully disprove Einstein's theory of relativity by propelling atoms faster than the speed of light. . . ." She trailed off. "What? Why are you looking at me like that?"

"Nothing. It's just crazy how much you remember."

"I can teach you the trick. Mrs. Candide, my second foster mom, said that when you're trying to memorize stuff you don't know, you should think of funny words you do know. Like when Einstein lists all the possible ways the world could end, I think of silly words, so Giant Atom Accelerator becomes 'giant angry alligator.' 'Asteroid collision' became 'aardvark constipation.'" Mia stopped abruptly. "Holy Gouda." She beckoned to Homer with one hand and pointed at the sky with the other. "Hurry, before he moves."

Homer moved to the side of the boat. With his shoulder pressed against the hull he could feel the wood vibrating from Mia's kicking heels. "Plane?" He looked up, trying to follow the line from Mia's pointed finger to the sky.

"No, silly." Mia nudged Homer toward the bow, turning him so that her swinging feet fell on either side of him. Her vanilla lotion made her smell like a cookie. "See? There's a sea turtle in the clouds."

Homer searched above. He saw white clouds and blue sky. But no turtle. "Wow. That's. Yeah. A turtle. I see it. Cool." Being around Mia had a way of reducing Homer's vocabulary to one-syllable words.

"Isn't it?" Mia stopped swinging her legs. "Yesterday, I found a piglet and an orangutan. Madame Quixote told me that that meant . . . Oh, eggs and biscuits. I can't remember." Mia pressed her thumbs to her face. "It wasn't a bad sign. It meant something good. Something lucky."

"Is Madame Quixote the one who tells fortunes by looking at the bottom of people's feet?"

"No, silly. That's Madame Avex. She's next to the Dollar-a-Slice. Madame Quixote has a card table under the yellow awning by the bumper cars. She reads your palm and tea leaves. Since I'm avoiding caffeine these days, it was palm reading or nothing." Mia looked down as she patted her stomach. "Right, Tadpole? You kick up a storm already. No use adding caffeine to the mix."

"I would miss coffee," Homer said, adding lamely, "if I was pregnant." His cheeks were warm before he finished speaking.

Mia tilted her head toward her left shoulder and stuck her lips out. Other people bit the sides of their mouths, scratched their heads, or did something else equally predictable, but Mia made a face like a fish when she was thinking. "Did you have something to tell me?"

"I'm supposed to remind you about the paving." Homer nudged a soda can in front of his left foot and then stepped on it, trying to shift his weight as slowly as possible to draw out the satisfying sound of crunching metal.

"Paving?"

"The lot. Tomorrow."

"Oh, right." Mia scooted back—left, right, left, right—until she could reach the mast and pull against it to stand. "Geeza Louisa. Getting up was so much easier without Tadpole on board."

"You can stay with us. My dads said to tell you. For, like, as long as you need. No problem."

"Okay." Mia looked down, met Homer's gaze, then looked at her interlaced fingers. Her unreadable expression might as well have been a punch in Homer's stomach.

"I'm sorry."

"You say 'sorry' way too much, Homer."

"Yeah. Sorry. Shit."

Mia shook her head. Her eyes were obscured by loose strands of red drifting across her face. "Tell your dads it's no big deal. I'll be okay."

"You sure? Because I can—"

"Yup. Well, I've got to get Tadpole some breakfast and finish my makeup. I'll be over in twenty."

"Great. Okay." If Homer had been a different person, he would have told her that she didn't need to wear makeup. He would have said, "You look amazing without it." But he wasn't a different person. He was only himself. So he nodded, waved, and walked out through the gate made of beautiful junk, across a cracked parking lot sprinkled with broken things.

THE PARABLE OF THE
ANYWHERE GIRL

BEFORE THEY KNEW HER NAME, they called
her the Anywhere Girl.

Her accent was unplaceable, untraceable. The hue of her
skin fell somewhere between wet driftwood and cold syrup.
Her features seemed shaped by a watercolor brush. When she
had rolled into town, her fingertips were still stained with the
dye she'd used to color her hair bright, plastic red. More often
than not, she smelled like burned sugar and warm clay.

"Pretty" wasn't the right word for her. "Beautiful"?
"Lovely"? Those didn't quite work either. She was another
word, a word that had not yet been made up.

People who claimed to remember her arrival on that June
day said they heard her before they saw her. According to some,
her truck had clicked and clacked like it had marbles in its
engine and the small sailboat it was pulling on a time-forgotten
trailer fought the twisted ropes tying it down. When she had

pulled into the lot at the end of the boardwalk, the truck had made a sound like a large man wheezing, then shuddered, and then died. Never to run again.

Between the strong push of the Caribbean winds and the powerful pull of the currents from the Gulf, the Island at the End of the World—or at least Florida—rarely had rainy days. But the morning after the Anywhere Girl's entrance, the sky darkened, the clouds thickened, and it poured for a week.

The first time the Anywhere Girl came into La Isla Souvenirs, she was barefoot and didn't say a word. The second time, she wore flip-flops that smacked against the wooden floor like she had flyswatters attached to her feet, and she didn't stop speaking until she had a job and a new pair of sunglasses.

The store's owners hired her without asking too many questions. It was only later that they thought to wonder, *Why did we do that?* Maybe it was how the small gap between her front teeth gave certain words a whistle or maybe it was the rambling way she spoke, jumping from topic to topic like a frog hopping from one rock to the next. Her thoughts were as tangled and disorderly as the new growth after a forest fire.

Within weeks of her starting at the store, foot traffic doubled. Tourists came back over and over because she had a way of calming cranky babies and coaxing surly preteens to smile. Lifeguards drifted in for suntan lotion and bottled water and often left with neither, but with a lot of stuff they hadn't meant to buy and definitely didn't need. The island's ancient bachelors, retired and aimless for years, came in to escape their loneliness and left feeling a little less lost. And the waiters and bartenders of Captain Toby's Seafood Palace made themselves late again and again for the night shift because they lost track of time trying to figure out the possible meanings of the Anywhere Girl's half dozen or so tattoos.

Was that a dragon on her left arm, or a flying horse?

How much had the turtle on her wrist hurt?

Could anyone read the words around her ankle?

Is that Greek or Arabic or neither or both?

By September, girls at the middle school were begging their parents to let them dye their hair Popsicle-colored shades. Clean feet were out. Bare feet were in. When a story twisted through town that the Anywhere Girl climbed out of her sailboat each night to skinny-dip in the moonlit sea, high schoolers, boys and girls alike, started sneaking out of windows and creeping down back staircases in order to gather in whispering circles along the dark ocean shore. They yawned their way through classes and never saw so much as a naked elbow.

After it became obvious that the Anywhere Girl was expecting a baby, so much speculation hummed in the air that the island's dogs howled for days. But the Anywhere Girl seemed oblivious to the gossip.

If asked directly about the baby's dad, the Anywhere Girl's answer was different every time: He was an astronaut on his way to settle Mars. A convict serving twenty to life. A former soap opera star who now spent all his time making weight-loss infomercials.

So what if her stories went in all directions at once? So what if her smile caused ice cream vendors to crash their carts and fishing boat captains to steer starboard when they meant to go port? So what if her enigmatic warmth pulled you in while at the same time something deep in her eyes kept you out? The Anywhere Girl didn't mean to hurt anyone. She didn't mean to cause any broken hearts. Like many a survivor of that particular anguish, the Anywhere Girl didn't want to inflict it on another, not if she could help it.

So she stayed friendly but unreachable. She laughed and became a part of each and every place she lived. But the Anywhere Girl always kept a few bags packed and postcards of towns with inviting names pinned to the wall by her bed, because imagining the possibilities of new places helped her fall into a deep, dreamless sleep.

THE NIGHT OF FIERY DESTRUCTION AND THE MORNING OF LIFE-CHANGING DECISIONS

THAT NIGHT, WHEN THE DOORBELL rang, Homer's first thought was to be surprised that he had fallen asleep at all. He'd been certain that his whirling brain wouldn't let him rest, not when it had the day's worries stuck on repeat.

Was Mia acting strange this afternoon? Sad?

Does she know she should stay on the island? With us? With me?

Why do I keep putting off college applications? Every day I do means it'll suck even more to do them later.

His second thought was that doorbells ringing late at night seldom equaled good news.

Homer crept out of his room past Einstein's closed door and down the stairs.

From the squeaky second step, Homer could see D.B. and Christian side by side in the entryway: one pale, tall, and slight; the other dark-skinned and broad shouldered. Both of them standing so straight and still, they looked every inch like the professional dancers they once were. Mr. Harvey was standing on the porch just outside the open door. It took a minute for Homer's foggy brain to process that the fire chief was dressed in the same stiff overalls and thick jacket he'd worn when he visited Homer's middle school on career day, and that the splash of red behind him wasn't a light or a flag on a passing boat: it was Mia's tangled hair.

Homer was so focused on shuffling quietly into the entryway that he only caught fragments of what D.B. was telling Chief Harvey.

"A miscommunication . . . no charges against Miss Márquez . . . safety class . . . after . . . baby . . . dance lessons . . ."

The conversation kept going, but for Homer the world went mute when Chief Harvey shifted his helmet to his left arm and gently guided Mia into the house with his right.

Her eyes were laced with red and she had stripes of soot across her face and arms. The black garbage bag she nudged inside with her feet didn't look like it contained very much at all.

Christian put an arm around Mia's shoulders and drew her farther inside, while D.B. nodded and smiled and said good-bye for a painfully long time before finally shutting the door.

"I'm so sorry. That was so, so, so, so stupid." Mia wiped her eyes against her arm, and when she raised her face she kept blinking as though she were trying to see through smoke. "I thought I was helping. I didn't know how else to get rid of a boat. And I was going to clean up after the fire." Mia's breath came out in gasps, and light reflected off the tears gathered in a pool above her lower lashes. She closed her eyes, bowed her head, and clenched her fists so tightly her knuckles turned white. "I'm sorry. Instead of making less trouble, I made more."

"Oh, you poor kid." Christian wrapped both arms around Mia, drawing her face as close to his chest as her stomach would allow. "Shhhh. It doesn't matter. It will be all right. It will be better than okay. It will be amazing."

Mia kept her palms pressed to her face and Christian started swaying side to side. *Just like he used to do when I had nightmares.* The thought made Homer wistful. *It'd be nice to be a kid again. Everything was simpler.*

Homer's eyes met D.B.'s. And even though he wasn't, when D.B. silently asked, "Are you okay?" Homer nodded yes. Then they both waited until Mia's sobs turned into hiccups and then stilled completely.

"Okay?" Christian asked, holding her at arm's length and studying her face.

Mia sniffled. "Uh-huh." She sniffled again and wiped her nose across her bare arm.

"You must be exhausted," D.B. said, grabbing Mia's garbage bag and moving down the hallway. "We'll set you up in the office. The pullout is ancient, but it should do for a night."

"Mia can have my room." Homer didn't mean to shout. The last thing he wanted was to wake up Einstein and have his little brother come down and ask Mia a million questions. When he spoke again, it was in a whisper. "The bathroom's easier to get to and the bed's bigger and stuff."

After a moment of silent consideration, Christian nodded, and D.B. handed Homer Mia's bag. When Mia looked at him, tears still glistening in her eyes, Homer knew that he would have spent the night in a puddle if it meant he could fall asleep and dream about the exact smile she had just given him.

By the time Homer found the extra toothbrushes in the bathroom that connected his room with Einstein's, Mia was already curled up in the center of his bed. Her eyes were shut and her bright hair fanned across her face and the navy sheets. He could see her breath rise and fall in her shoulder blades and make out the fragile curve of her spine through the T-shirt he'd given her to sleep in. Even with her baby bump, the shirt still came to Mia's knees.

Homer set the toothbrush by the alarm clock on the bedside table and tried to balance on his tiptoes as he walked. He had one foot in the hall when Mia's drowsy voice stopped him.

"Hey, Homer?"

He turned around. "Yeah?"

Mia, her eyes still closed, adjusted her head higher on the pillow. "Three questions: What was the worst part of the day, what was the best part of the day, and what"—she yawned—"would you do differently?"

"Do you mean for me, my day, or the day in general?" Homer felt an echoing yawn pull at the corners of his mouth.

"I mean your day, silly," Mia said, smiling into the pillow. "My favorite sister, Dotts. She's the one—"

"You met Dotts at the first place you lived after leaving your mom's 'for real.'" Homer took a deep breath and continued. "And you liked Dotts so much that you asked to go with her when she got moved to Mrs. Scott's—the house of the foster mom with the French bulldog that peed on your backpack and chewed Dotts's sneakers."

"I talk about her a lot, huh?" Mia opened her eyes.

Homer shrugged. "She probably talks about you just as much."

Mia stared at him in a way that Homer couldn't quite place: her eyes a blend of awe and sadness. Then she shook her head and the look was gone.

"Any-who. Dotts and I would play Three Questions if one of the new kids couldn't sleep or if someone was scared or if Mr. Scott was home and Mrs. Scott was yelling and we didn't want to leave our bedroom." She nodded toward Homer. "Gentlemen first."

"Okay." Homer struggled to herd his thoughts. "Worst? That's easy. Your boat, I mean your house, getting destroyed because I didn't—"

"It's not your fault," Mia interrupted. "Next question. Best?"

"That you're safe, I guess."

"You're the sweetest. Differently?"

"I would have explained about the lot better?"

"Hey," Mia said indignantly. "Those were all about me, not you."

Homer tilted his head. "Sorry. That's all I've got. Your turn."

"Fine, but you owe me three not-about-me answers." Mia shut her eyes again. "Best? Tadpole kicked up a storm today. I think she or he likes watermelon. Worst?" She exhaled. "I forgot my best pen in the boat. And I got D.B. and Christian in trouble with Chief Harvey."

"It'll be fine. I'm pretty sure Christian has Chief and Mrs. Harvey in his Beginning Ballroom class at the Rec. You can't be upset with someone who's showing you how to waltz."

Mia smiled sleepily. "You're funny, Homer."

"Not really."

"Someday, you're going to have to learn how to take a compliment." Mia yawned again. "Would you get the postcard from my bag?"

"Sure." Homer started rummaging through Mia's black garbage bag of possessions. "Only one? What happened to all the others you had around your bed?"

Mia's response sounded like she was speaking through a mask. "Dwidn't nweed'dem."

Homer's fingers grazed a cardboard rectangle. "Is this it?" He turned the card to look at the picture. It showed a beach at dusk. The sand wasn't white like it was on La Isla de Plátanos and the water was black instead of turquoise, but there was a dark peacefulness to the sculpted sand dunes and frosted waves. "Glory-Be-by-the-Sea," Homer read, then added, "It looks pretty."

"That's where I'm going to live. With Dotts. She'll be so, so happy to see me. She has an apartment and a job and a boyfriend who buys her flowers. . . ." Mia's voice trailed off.

"But you have a job *here*." Homer felt like he was trying to breathe underwater. "And I read somewhere that people shouldn't fly in the last three months of pregnancy," he added, cringing at how his desperation clung to every syllable.

"I'm not flying. No way. The bus isn't so bad. Sometimes you can even get two seats all to yourself." Mia rolled so her back was again to Homer. "I'm gonna go to sleep now."

"Okay." Homer didn't trust himself to say much more, but after turning off the light and pulling the door nearly shut, he remembered something. "Mia?"

"Uh-huh?"

"You never said what you'd do differently."

"Hmmm," Mia hummed into her pillow. "I would have brought marshmallows."

Homer smiled and gently pulled the door all the way closed.

"Aren't you supposed to sleep until noon during your *last* high school winter break? You keep this up, I'll have to ask Einstein to tutor you in Being a Teenager 101."

Homer lifted his forehead off the kitchen table just enough to be able to see D.B. leaning in the kitchen doorway. "It's a little early for sarcasm, don't you think?"

"That depends. Are you being sarcastic?" D.B. stretched his arms above his head, reaching for the ceiling. Even when he rose to his tiptoes, he was a couple of inches shy of reaching it. "Ugh. You kids are making me shrink. I used—"

"To be six feet tall and able to float like a feather. So you've said." Homer folded his arms on the table and rested his cheek on them. "I made coffee."

"I know. I could smell it from down the hall." D.B. shuffled toward the French press and the mugs Homer had set up on the counter. His brown-and-gray hair was flat on one side of his head, while on the other it stuck out at all angles. When he turned around, his expression had changed completely. "Wow. It took me until this moment to remember: Mia set her boat on fire. You slept on the sofa bed. Shit." D.B. rubbed at his eyes. "The universe needs to give that kid a break." He dropped his hands. "Please don't tell your other dad I said 'shit.'"

"Oh, I won't." Homer wanted to say something more, but his sleep-deprived brain wouldn't let him pull together the right words. Even when D.B. was stressed or angry or disappointed, he kept a hint of his regular smile in his eyes. Homer could count on two hands the number of times he'd seen his dad unhappy.

"Want a cup?" D.B. held up the French press.

"Sure," Homer said. "Thanks."

D.B. slid a mug with a dancing plantain on one side and "Life Is Bonita on La Isla de Plátanos" on the other across the table to Homer, and followed that up with the carton of cream and the sugar bowl. Then he sat in the chair directly across from Homer and added cream and sugar to his own mug. D.B. was so lost in his thoughts that he didn't notice the rings his overflowing mug had left across the table or the coffee that dripped off the mug's handle onto his T-shirt. Or maybe he did notice and just didn't care.

"Mia fall asleep okay?"

"I think so. We talked for a few minutes, but she started yawning, so I left her alone." Homer reached for the sugar and added a spoonful to his mug. He didn't normally drink sweet coffee, but he needed something to do with his hands.

"Homes, has Mia mentioned anything to you about her plans?"

Homer looked up from his twirling spoon. D.B. was leaning toward him, his arms crossed on the table, everything about his expression and posture demonstrating what a great dad he was. Warm, generous, and caring. *How did I get so lucky?* The thought should have filled Homer with gratitude, but that morning it flooded him with guilt. *It's not fair. Why did I get my dads and Mia didn't get anyone?*

"Homes? Burn your tongue?"

D.B.'s voice was so full of concern that Homer felt tempted

to tell his dad what he'd been thinking ever since the day Mia found out she was pregnant. *Maybe if I explain, D.B. could help.* But then Christian walked into the kitchen and Homer was glad that he hadn't said a thing.

"Morning," said Christian, moving toward the counter, one hand already reaching for the coffeepot. "Oh, *gewd. Cue-feee.*"

Homer had woken from a fitful sleep to the sound of Christian video chatting with his brother and sisters in Cape Town. These hours-long conversations always left his dad with a refreshed accent. Normally, Homer would tease him about his funny vowels and clinking sounds, but at that moment, he didn't have the energy.

"It's strong," D.B. said, turning. "You've taught our first-born well."

"Homer made it?" Christian asked. "Up so early? Did I wake you with the video call? Your uncle Amahle is so loud and I forgot you were sleeping in the office. Did you sleep at all?" Christian slid into the chair nearest the door, his hands wrapped tightly around his green-and-white AmaZulu Football Club mug.

Homer closed his eyes and let the steam from his coffee drift against his eyelids. The warmth felt amazing. "Can I finish this cup before we play Twenty Questions?" He opened his eyes and sat up straighter.

"C.," D.B. said before Christian could answer, "Homer and I were talking about Mia's situation."

"Yes. Of course." Christian looked from D.B. to Homer and back again. "David, you should make sure to tell her again that she's welcome to stay. I think if she keeps hearing it from both of us, she might actually consider."

"I've told her. Many times."

Homer cleared his throat, sat up straighter, and then spoke. "Mia told me she was going to go stay with her foster sister, the one she's always talking about."

"Dotty?" Christian asked.

"Dotts," Homer corrected. "She lives almost at the tip of Cape Cod now. Mia said she would take the bus, but I was thinking I could drive her."

For a moment, the only sounds in the kitchen were the noises that drifted in through the open window over the sink: the clank of metal storefront gates rising, the rattle of ice cream carts being pulled on the beach, and the screech of seagulls gearing up for another day of snatching unprotected food.

D.B. was the first to speak. "That's a long drive, Homes."

"I know, but I could make it up and back before Christmas if we leave in a couple of days. I could meet you guys at Grandma's. Maybe even get to Mobile a little early."

"Homer." D.B. pressed his palms flat against the table and leaned forward in such a way that Homer could see the patches of gray hair on the top of his head. "It's out of the question. For starters, you've never traveled on your own."

"That's more of an argument for why I should go." Homer

decided to play his final card. "What if I want to go to college out of state? Driving Mia to Massachusetts would give me the chance to see other parts of the country. The farthest north I've ever been is Alabama. That's not the kind of traveling you can write about in an application essay."

"You have plenty to write about, Homer. You live on an island. You have two dads. Your brother's a genius, albeit one who's obsessed with the end of the world—"

"D.B., none of that stuff is about me. It's about geography and why my family's interesting and I'm not."

"That's not true. What about—"

Christian interrupted. "David, this might not be a bad idea."

"Really?" Homer couldn't keep the surprise out of his voice.

"This trip could be a good introduction to"—Christian paused, considering his words carefully—"places beyond the island. Plus, he'd be doing something nice for a young lady who we all care about deeply."

"Homes, you think you're up for this?" The pause between "Homes" and the rest of D.B's question was heavy with worry, love, and uncertainty.

Homer nodded. Then he shook his head. Finally, he shrugged. "I don't know. But I want to find out."

"Wise words," said Christian, wrapping his hands around D.B.'s. "Ali Isley's wife takes salsa lessons from me. He'll give me a deal on a car. Homer and Mia have phones. And it'll be good for Homer and Einstein to do some bonding. Steiner spends way too much time taking classes with kids almost twice his age."

Homer's heart sank, but before he could protest, Einstein shambled into the room. "I'll accept your proposition on one condition," he said, stumbling when his left foot caught the bottom of his too-long pajama pants.

"Did you know he was there?" D.B. asked, looking at Christian.

"Of course. The perk of sitting by the door: you can see right to the end of the hall, and Einstein was much closer than that." Christian leaned back in his chair and took a sip of coffee. "All right, what's the condition?"

"That after Homer and I drop off Mia, we drive to the town of Grace Mountains, New Hampshire, and I get to attend the second annual I-9 Institute for the Study of Probable Doom, Existential Risks, and Apocalyptic Possibilities Conference on the Significant Dangers and Slim Rewards of the Giant Atom Accelerator."

Christian sat up. "Can you explain that in plain English?"

Einstein took a deep breath. "I'd like to attend an educational two-day conference where the greatest scientist in the world will speak about the ways that a test run of a very, very big machine that is designed to make atoms go very, very fast could cause the destruction of life as we know it on December twentieth at eleven fifty-nine p.m."

"Not exactly an uplifting topic," Christian said, frowning.

Einstein crossed his arms. "My offer ensures that I will not spend the majority of my winter break either begging you for rides to the university labs or shutting myself in my room and listening to Apollo Aces's new album at the highest possible volume on a stereo system that I have modified to achieve a decibel level of one hundred and fifteen, which is just five decibels shy of the sound level at a rock concert. Do you accept my terms?"

"I accept." Homer raised his hand. "If taking Einstein to a nerd convention means we can go, I accept."

D.B. hunched his shoulders. Homer thought he was trying not to laugh, but when he spoke it sounded more like he was trying not to cry. "Okay."

"Okay?" asked Homer.

"Okay." D.B. stood up and walked his dancer's walk, heel to toe, across the kitchen. When he got to the doorframe, he rapped his knuckles against the bright-blue surface. *Tap. Tap. Tap.* "There'll be rules. You're going to call every day. I want an itinerary. And . . . I'll think of the rest."

"Okay," Homer said.

"Okay," D.B. said. "Now, I just need a minute to . . ." His voice trailed off as he disappeared down the hall.

At the sound of the front door slapping shut, Christian turned around from watching D.B. leave and fixed his eyes on a deep scratch in the table. Any hint of the smile he'd had during Einstein's presentation was gone. "Don't worry. Your dad will be himself in a bit. He's very protective. He has reasons to be."

"Like what?" said Einstein, "It's not like Homer and I get in trouble—ever."

"Most places aren't like the island. The real world"—Christian made air quotes on "real world"—"isn't as accepting of people who don't fit its models. Many people see 'different' as a danger. This scares them." Christian pressed two fingers to the space between his eyes. "When people get scared, they do stupid things. Some get mean. Some angry. Some violent. Your dad experienced all three." Christian sighed as he stood up. "But those are his stories to tell you someday."

"Okay." Homer had more questions, but he held them in.

Christian yawned, stretching his arms above his head. "Why don't you two go tell Mia the plan, if she's awake."

Einstein waited until Christian had walked beyond the kitchen and out of sight before he spoke. "You really think the way to get Mia to stay here is to drive her eighteen hundred miles away?"

"How'd you—"

Einstein held up his hands like he was surrendering a weapon. "Homes, you're about as opaque as a beaker—and you left your list of 'Ideas to Convince Mia' open on the living room computer. You'll need to add this one: 'Take a very, very, very long road trip.'"

Normally, Einstein's egomaniac-professor voice would have made Homer laugh, but today he was too tired and nervous. "I've got to try something."

"To quote the great astrophysicist Stephen Hawking, 'Things cannot make themselves impossible.' Not even one-sided love." Einstein patted his brother's arm as he left the kitchen. "I added that last part. Good luck. You're going to need it."

Homer waited until he was alone to respond.

"I know."

THE PARABLE OF THE ORDINARY GUY (WHO JUST WANTED SOMETHING TO BELIEVE IN)

THE ORDINARY GUY WAS a newspaper without cartoons. He was unflavored oatmeal and caffeine-free diet soda. He was an earth-toned T-shirt paired with stainproof khakis. The human equivalent of waiting in line at a post office or reading through the fine print of a terms-and-conditions agreement.

In other words . . .

He was uninteresting.

He was boring.

He was sheltered and naive.

He was ordinary.

Once upon a time, the Ordinary Guy hadn't been aware of his unspectacular state. Indeed, he didn't realize until ninth grade—when he hit his third growth spurt—how remarkably unremarkable he was. In high school, suddenly the same kids he'd been in classes with since kindergarten wanted to stick out instead of blend in. They were competing for superlatives while fighting the status quo.

The Best soccer player!

The Smartest class president!

The Greatest artist!

Even being *The Worst!* at something was considered a kind of achievement.

At first, the Ordinary Guy aspired to be interesting. He tried on different selves as though they were T-shirts from a sales rack—but none of them quite fit. Freshman year, he joined (and left) almost every club at Plátanos High: debate, poetry, robotics, et cetera. Sophomore year, he *really* put an effort into liking sports—soccer and baseball, specifically—but realized that being just good enough to make JV meant he spent most of his time sitting on a bench or shading his eyes in the outfield. By the spring of the Ordinary Guy's junior year, he just about gave up on "interesting."

And then a *very* interesting girl with an amazing face and a generous heart came into his life, and due to a crack in the cosmos, a wobble in the Earth's rotation, divine pity raining from the heavens, or some similarly fantastical reason, she thought the Ordinary Guy was a lot of things he wasn't: funny, smart, talented, and (possibly) charming.

Unfortunately, the fact that this extraordinary girl made the Ordinary Guy feel better than ordinary—special, even—didn't solve all his problems. Rather, this friendship created a new complication. For it should be recognized as a natural law that the difficulty of making decisions about the future is directly proportional to the amount of internal entropy created by love.

The Ordinary Guy concluded that what he needed was a change of place. A shake-up of geography. Of the predictable. The routine.

Save for his heart—as the saying goes—the Ordinary Guy had nothing to lose.

ON THE ROAD TO GLORY
OR DISASTER

WHEN HOMER WOKE UP THE morning of December twelfth, the weak ribbons of daylight that slipped between the window blinds were still two feet away from reaching the office carpet. He had hours before anyone else in the house would be awake, but falling back asleep was impossible.

Homer stared at the water stain on the ceiling and tried to think about logistics. *Did I pack enough T-shirts? Should I get more deodorant? Do the red sneakers smell better than my running shoes?* It wasn't long, however, before his mind turned to Mia.

Sometimes, he thought about random things, like how her smile stretched across her whole face in a way that made it impossible not to smile back and how amazing her hair looked when thick clouds pressed the humidity against the earth and the dense air made all the strands around her face curl. How the muscles in her legs popped when she walked in sand. How smooth the skin in the dip between her shoulder blades would feel under his fingertips.

Other times, his thoughts led him to places he didn't like to go. To remembering how much he liked her and how sometimes liking her hurt even more than being caught in a riptide.

Homer picked up a throw pillow and pressed it to his face, silently repeating, *She's pregnant. She doesn't feel the same. She's pregnant. She doesn't feel the same.* Soon the sentences became garbled: *She feel pregnant. Same doesn't she's.*

The fact that Homer hadn't gotten much sleep the past three nights was definitely not helping him control his brain.

The morning light was still over a foot from reaching the office carpet, but Homer couldn't lie on the lumpy mattress any longer. He got to his feet and pulled on a T-shirt, thinking as he folded the bed back into a sofa, *Holy shit. We're leaving. Today.*

Mia and Einstein were already outside when Homer heard tires crunching on the gravel driveway, followed by a horn that sounded like a flock of mournful ducks quacking.

Time's up. Homer didn't bother trying to zip up his overstuffed bag. He flung the straps over his shoulder, took one final look around his room, and then pounded down the steps and out to the porch, where he found Mia and Einstein staring straight ahead with their mouths slightly open.

"Hey, what are you— Oh, wow." Homer stopped by the front railing. "So that's it?"

"Indeed," Einstein said, his expression puzzled, like he'd

heard the punch line but missed the joke.

"Well," Mia said, turning her head to the side as though she was trying to get a better angle. "It's certainly . . . yellow."

"Yup," said Homer.

"That it is," said Einstein.

All three of them stared, silently watching Christian as he used an old T-shirt to polish the dashboard, the steering wheel, and any other place he could reach from the driver's seat.

"The banana . . . hood ornament thingie . . . ," Mia continued haltingly. "I think it *could* grow on me. On *us*. If we try really, really hard."

"It will be hard," said Homer.

"Exorbitantly," said Einstein.

Silence.

"Soooo." Mia wiggled her toes in a wave—one way, then the other. "Christian looks happy. He must have gotten a good deal."

"I hope he did," said Homer.

"I concur," said Einstein.

More silence.

"We could call it the Banana-mobile. You know? Because of the color—and the hood ornament." Mia put her hands on her hips. "The thing is, I can't decide if I hate it or love it." She pressed a finger to her lips, considering her options. "I love it. The yellow grew on me."

"That quickly?" Homer asked.

"Yup. Yup. Yup." Mia took one step per "yup" as she hopped down from the porch. "Christian, are the cup holders big enough for Slurpees? Tadpole loves, loves, loves Slurpees." She did a funny walk-jog-skip to the yellow car and then circled it, running one hand over the bright paint while Christian, from the inside, pointed and gave explanations that Homer couldn't hear.

Homer, his raised left eyebrow a silent question, glanced at his brother.

Einstein shrugged in response. "Maybe it has an excellent fuel efficiency rating."

"Okay." Homer picked up his bag. "Let's check it out and load up the rest of the stuff." He and Einstein were halfway down the front walk when the screen door screeched open behind them.

"Few more safety items," D.B. said, nodding at the two cardboard boxes he held balanced in his arms. "Extra bandages, more of Einstein's Lac-Fab pills, road flares, that kind of thing." He walked down the stairs two at a time and hurried toward the car's trunk as if he were afraid Homer or Einstein would protest the additional boxes.

"You guys ready to go?" Christian slammed the driver's-side door shut and clapped his hands together as he walked toward the house. He stopped and put an arm around Einstein's shoulders. "Would you believe I only paid Ali one thousand dollars for this?"

"Not sure 'only' is the right word," Einstein mumbled.

Mia had made her way back toward the house slowly, as though she was worried about interrupting. But when she reached Christian and flung her arms around his neck, all hesitancy vanished. "Thank you. It's a great car. Thank you so much, for everything. This has been the best place I've ever lived."

"Really?" D.B. said before he slammed the trunk hard enough to make the whole ugly, yellow car rattle. He still had to press down and jump on the lid before it clicked shut. "Jesus." He wiped an arm across his forehead. "The trunk hinges need some oil or nonstick spray or something." He circled around the side of the car to stand in front of Christian. "Mia, I have to say it one more time. If you get lonely up there or overwhelmed, Christian and I would love to have you."

"I know," Mia said, stepping out of Christian's hug and vigorously shaking her head. "And I can't thank you enough for everything you all have done for me. You've been crazy generous." She shaded her eyes and stared so intently toward the place where the white sand of the beach met the turquoise water that Homer knew she was committing it to memory. "It's so beautiful here, but I think Glory-Be-by-the-Sea is going to be great. Me and Dotts, we're going to help each other. I'll get a job. Maybe take some classes. We'll get books and read to Tadpole." Mia circled her arms around D.B.'s waist. "It will be super."

D.B. caught Homer's eye. He smiled knowingly and wiped his eyes on his left arm while he hugged Mia back with his right. As soon as she stepped away, D.B. pulled Homer and Einstein into a hug so tight, Homer felt like his nose was getting pushed in. "I'm going to miss you two so much." His extra squeeze on "so" caused Homer's elbow to press against Einstein's right cheek.

"Ow. That hurts." Einstein wiggled back and forth until his face was no longer smashed quite so much against Homer's arm.

"Yes." D.B. sighed loudly, but his usual levity was back. "Love does hurt, son. You don't need to be a genius to know that." D.B. shifted from side to side, leading Homer and Einstein in a slow circle.

"Oh, why are these here?" D.B. dropped his arms. Homer took a grateful breath as he turned around to see Mia standing by the open passenger-side door, a plastic-wrapped rectangle held above her head. "There's like a gazillion of them in here."

D.B. clapped his hands. "Disposable cameras. I thought they'd come in handy."

Einstein must have given D.B. some kind of look, because he threw his arms up with exaggerated exasperation. "Come on. Disposable cameras are a thing again. They're hip. Cool. Off the heezy. The bomb diggity."

"Please stop," Einstein interrupted. "I'm socially inept, and you trying to be cool makes *me* feel awkward."

D.B. rolled his eyes. "Now that I feel my age, you kids need to take off before I have an old-man meltdown. Homer, you'll call every night?"

Homer nodded.

"What are you waiting for, then?" Christian put an arm around D.B.'s shoulders and tossed a single key on a ring with a pineapple charm to Homer. "Get on the road. Go crazy. Have fun. Be happy."

"Be safe," D.B. said, his eyebrows pinched as if he were trying to remember something else he meant to say. "And be kind to people—even if they're not kind to you."

Homer pressed the sharp side of the key against his thumb. "Okay," he said, throwing his bag into the back of the bright-yellow car and then sliding into the driver's seat. "We'll see you soon." He waited until Mia and Einstein closed their doors and clicked their seat belts before he shifted the most hideous vehicle in the world into drive.

NOT AS IT WAS PLANNED, BUT AS IT MUST BE

THE FIRST DAY, THEY DIDN'T even make it out of Florida. The first night, they stayed at La Mancha Magnífico Motel. It was not magnificent—quite the opposite actually.

Homer and Einstein's room smelled like the inside of an abandoned gym bag. Neither one of them slept under the suspiciously stained comforter on his bed, and Einstein put grocery bags over his feet before stepping into the narrow shower. Mia's room reeked of cheap air freshener and cooked eggs, but she said Tadpole must like the smell because he or she was kicking like a ninja all night.

The second day started slowly. The three of them loaded luggage into the car like the bags had been stuffed with bowling balls during the night. Mia, who swore that she'd never liked coffee anyway, took a few sips from Homer's third cup at La Mancha Magnífico Motel's sad excuse for a free continental breakfast.

When they got back on the highway, Homer's view from the passenger-side window was a slide show set on replay: subdivision, subdivision, splash of green, superstore, eighteen-wheeler, tollbooth, and repeat. The car didn't have a CD player, never mind a place to hook up a phone, and the leather seats emitted an odor not unlike fruit left too long in the sun. The fact that the windows had to be rolled down with plastic handles didn't help with the stale-air situation.

Homer spent much of the morning lost in his own head, hypnotized by the unexciting view and his worrying, until Mia broke into his reverie.

"Homer?"

"Sorry. What?"

"Homer." Mia stretched out his name to twice its length. *Hommmerrrr.* "What'd I tell you about saying 'sorry' so much?"

"It's his favorite word," Einstein said over the pings and booms of whatever game he was playing on his handheld.

"No it's not." Homer turned to look at his brother. They were only a few hours into the second day of the trip, but somehow Einstein had already made the backseat look like Los Plátanos Pier the morning after a festival. Food wrappers and soda cans were piled on the passenger-side floor, various science magazines were splayed across the seats, and a small mountain of clothes dominated the space behind Mia. "Jesus, Steiner. Make yourself at home. Why do you have boxers on the floor?"

"I don't know about you"—Einstein glanced up from his

game—"but I like to be prepared. Great. There goes my last life." He dropped his player on the seat. "The world's going to end in seven days and I'll never have made it past level six."

"Don't feel bad." Mia looked over her shoulder. "One of my—"

Beeeeeeeeeeeeeep. The driver of a delivery van kept his horn pressed until Mia jerked the car back into the right lane.

"Oops," Mia shouted at her closed window like she thought the delivery guy could hear her. "*Lo siento.* Anyway, when I lived with the Gardiners—they're the family with two bio kids and a rabbit named Shiloh—two foster boys, twins actually, came in the last month I was there and one of them, Tucker, wet his pants sometimes even though he was eight. Mrs. Gardiner told me he'd grow out of it and to stop babying him." Mia frowned. "She was one of the bad eggs. Phew. I made sure Tucker had a clean pair of underwear in his backpack. I told him it was a secret." Mia smiled. "He liked that. I think it made him feel special. I'd put the new pair in a plastic lunch container just in case anyone peeked in. Maybe you should do that, Steiner."

If anyone else in the world had told his genius little brother to carry a spare pair of boxers in Tupperware, Homer would have been waiting for the punch line, but Mia's expression was earnest, her voice kind. *She'd probably give a dictator her last tissue if he had a cold.*

"Uh, okay. Thank you for the suggestion, Mia," Einstein

said, shifting forward so his knees touched the back of Homer's seat. "But I don't wet my pants."

"It's okay." Mia reached back to pat Einstein's leg, but he was too far on the passenger side for her to touch. "Tucker was embarrassed, too."

"No, I swear, the only reason I have underwear out is because if the Giant Atom Accelerator goes off early, I want to die wearing clean boxers." Einstein's protest was punctuated by squeaks from the backseat springs

Homer rolled his eyes. "You're telling us that in the *highly* unlikely event that an experiment in a can buried miles beneath the ground causes a ginormous black hole, you believe you're going to have time to change your underwear before the afore-mentioned black hole swallows the Earth?"

"First, it's the Giant Atom Accelerator, not a can," Einstein said, flopping back against the seat and crossing his arms. "Second, it would take me days to explain the effect a black hole could have on the properties of time in this dimension."

"Oh, we have time," Mia said. Homer turned around just quickly enough to catch her making her thinking-guppy face as she tried to see the road hidden by the driver's-side blind spot. "In fact-ta-roo, I'm going to get off the highway, because if I see one more minivan doing eighty, I will go bananas. Sorry, Banana." Mia patted the steering wheel. "We can take some small roads and Einstein can explain science stuff." She pointed at her stomach. "This way, Tadpole will grow up to be super,

super smart. And then we can stop for lunch and then we can find a camping ground because we have the nifty tents."

"No way. Those tents smell like melted crayons." Einstein snorted. "I don't think the dads have ever actually used them."

"Oh." Mia's expression changed so quickly, she looked almost like an entirely different person. Or maybe it wasn't the change so much as the shock of seeing her look unhappy. Most people's most-of-the-time faces were neutral: their lips neither curved up nor curved down, their eyes neither shining nor dull. But Mia was different. Her most-of-the-time face was dimples showing, lips slightly parted, and eyes open like she was afraid of missing something.

"S.F., Steiner," Homer said.

"How was that a social fail?" Einstein demanded, but then he must have caught Mia's reflection in a window. "Oh, we can go camping. Sounds like"—Einstein's eyes met Homer's in the side-view mirror—"fun."

Homer nodded. "Good job," he mouthed.

"I've never been camping," Mia said as she clicked on the blinker and pulled onto the exit ramp. Her voice was already a little brighter. "And I really do want Tadpole to be smarter."

"Smarter?" Einstein said. "Than me?" His tone was marked by disbelief, but Homer figured he'd just called him out on a social fail, so he'd let this one slide.

"Smart. I meant smart. I can't believe this song is on again. I love, love, love, love it." Mia turned the volume knob 180 degrees to the right. She started humming, then glanced at Homer. "New rule. If you're driving, you get to control the radio."

"That hardly seems—" But Homer's protest was drowned out by pop music as Mia turned the volume even louder and belted out her own off-key version of an already terrible song.

> *"Oh. Oh. Maybe tonight is the last song of this life.*
> *Oh, tonight's da, da, da, da song of our lives."*

Three hours later, while Homer and Mia switched seats, Einstein asked the two women smoking in lawn chairs by the Whistle and Pop Convenience Store entrance about local campgrounds. The smaller woman looked at him suspiciously, but the other one told him the only one open this time of year was two towns over, in a "hoot" of a place called Pythia Springs.

Not long after they got back on the road, the radio began to cut in and out, the signal turning to pure static when they reached the first sign: a massive billboard with two rows of gold-tinted spotlights, one above and one below. The whole thing shone like it had been dipped in plastic, and the color and font of the message made it sound less like an invitation and more like a demand: "Visit Pythia Springs, Home of the World-Famous American Oracle."

"I haven't seen that movie," Mia said in her singsong voice as she continued to focus on the intricate pattern of leaves, vines, and flowers she was doodling on her left forearm. She'd been drawing for the better part of an hour, starting at her wrist and working her way up to her elbow.

Einstein shook his head vigorously. "It's not a movie." He paused, glancing at Mia's homemade tattoo. "All that copper phthalocyanine can't be good for your skin."

"Aren't you sweet, worrying about me." Mia twisted and reached between her headrest and seat to pat the top of Einstein's hair.

Homer hadn't been jealous of Einstein in years, but something about Mia's easy affection for his brother lit a match in his chest. It burned for a moment, then went out, leaving a different feeling behind: shame. *He's your brother, you idiot. He stayed up past eleven to help you with your seventh-grade science fair project.* Homer whispered the thoughts. Even in his own mind, he didn't want them any louder.

"American Oracle," Mia said as she leaned toward the windshield, squinting at a sandwich board sign set up just before a bend in the road. "Three miles."

"Okay," said Homer, gripping the steering wheel much tighter than he needed to. "This is getting a little weird. You sure we have to camp here?"

"The nice lady said it was the only place open in December." Mia held her arm up, admiring her artwork. "What do you guys think of Pythia as a name for a girl, or Oracle for a boy?"

"Uh, I—"

"Brake!" Einstein yelled.

Homer slammed his foot on the brake pedal without thinking, bringing the Banana to a stop less than a foot from the bumper of the SUV in front of them. The air instantly smelled like hot rubber, and the Banana's engine cranked and sputtered before shutting down completely. Homer felt like his heart could break the bones of his rib cage, it was pounding so hard. "Everyone okay?"

"Phew, Homer." Mia pushed herself off the dashboard and sank back into her seat. "Good thing I had names ready, because if you'd slammed those brakes even a smidgen harder, Tadpole might have shot right out of me."

Homer couldn't tell whether Mia was being serious or joking. *Probably should assume "not joking."* "Sorry. I wasn't paying attention."

"What's with all the cars?" Einstein asked, pointing between the front seats.

Homer looked forward. A line of cars, vans, and trucks stretched in front of the Banana. The lights from countless brakes tapping on and off reminded Homer of blinking Christmas lights. Before he could think of a response to Einstein's question, the cars that had rolled in behind him started honking. It took three tries, and some mumbled swears under Homer's breath, but the Banana's engine finally caught and they rolled forward, just one more car in a caravan.

The dark woods that lined the road eventually gave way to run-down, abandoned buildings, each uniquely neglected and sad in its own way. The first one, a former gas station, resembled an unevenly baked cake. The hoses from the two pumps stretched across the crumbling asphalt like emaciated snakes, and the triangles of glass that framed the smashed windows and rusted door of Pythia's Finest Convenience Store were pointed teeth in a gaping mouth, revealing the empty shelves, cracked floor, and debris within.

A Victorian house two blocks after the gas station had railings leading up to the front door, but no steps. The rusted letters on a rotting sign propped against a tree stump read "Pythia Springs Inn," but the way that kudzu vines reached out of the windows like a giant squid's arms made it clear that it'd been a long time since the inn had had any guests.

The redbrick library was missing one of its four walls, the open side displaying piles of moldering books, chairs with missing legs, and toppled shelves. The building across the street from this diorama must once have been a church, but now it had a tree poking through a hole in the roof. Most of the other buildings were impossible to categorize because weather, neglect, and time had eroded their purposes.

"This place is so . . . lost," Mia whispered. She shook her head. "That's stupid. It doesn't make any sense."

"No," Homer replied. "'Lost' is as good a word as any."

At the same time, Homer thought "lost" wasn't quite enough. It was a forgotten place. A place saturated with old sadness.

The disarray made the next sign seem even more garish than

the first billboard they'd passed. "Welcome to Pythia Springs, South Carolina. Home of the American Oracle. Park Here." A giant arrow at the bottom pointed to a parking lot that was easily three times the size of the largest one Homer had ever seen. It was a field of black—the asphalt so new it glistened like it was still cooling to solid. Men and women wearing fluorescent-orange vests waved cars into rows and directed the vehicles' occupants to the sidewalk, to join the river of people all flowing in the same direction. Homer ignored the turn-here gesture of the fluorescent-vest man at the entrance and kept driving straight. He didn't know where he was going, but he knew it wasn't there.

The part of town after the billboard was as different from the one they'd driven through before as a palm tree is from a dandelion. *The buildings look like they were glued together from kits,* Homer thought. *More like a movie set than a place that's meant to last.*

"Wow." Mia pressed her nose against her window. "This part is worse than the first one."

Homer nodded. Mia was right. This neighborhood was too shiny, too new and too tame compared to the other. It was an amusement park next door to a graveyard.

Homer slowed the Banana to a crawl in front of a one-story clapboard house with a lawn sign that read "American Oracle. Tickets Here" and "10 a.m. Readings = $10. 3 p.m. is $15." This was the place where the river of people stopped and became solid, turning into a line of waiting ice cubes instead of moving water.

The man standing by the door with a clipboard and the woman taking people's cash at a plastic card table both wore bright, angular suits. In contrast, the four men and one woman smoking next to a huge SUV with tinted windows all had on torn jeans and misshapen T-shirts. The shiny black equipment piled on the sidewalk next to the van looked expensive, and apart from the three film cameras, Homer had no idea what it was.

A mile or so past the ticket house, the road turned to broken asphalt, then dirt, and then the faded sign for the Pythia Springs Campground and Motor Court appeared.

When Mia skipped back from the front office, which was housed in a small log cabin, she had a pile of complimentary mints cupped in her hands and a smile on her face. They were the only guests there, other than a long-term renter. The owner said that they could pick whatever site they wanted.

Homer both was and wasn't surprised.

"Is it supposed to look like that?" The pine needles and twigs under Mia's bare feet crunched as she shifted to her left, tilting her head like a curious bird. "I thought tents looked more like triangles."

"They do," Homer huffed from inside the tent as he watched Einstein's silhouette struggle to thread a long pole through plastic loops on the outside. "This one is just not cooperating." Homer sat back on his heels. Between the thick forest canopy and the quick rise of dusk, he could only sort of make out the faded instructions sewn on the pocket by the door. "Steiner, are you sure you're using the size-seven poles? Ow."

The pole Einstein had been working with hit Homer's left shoulder, and before he could react the front of the tent collapsed, enveloping him in waxy canvas. Homer could only imagine how ridiculous he looked as he fought his way under the suffocating fabric to the door. But when he breathed in the fresh air, he almost didn't care.

"Wait! Don't move, Homer," Mia shouted, reaching through the Banana's open passenger side window. She held one of the disposable cameras over her head like a torch and started clicking away. "Okay, now look mad." *Click.* "Now try sad." *Click.* "Happy." *Click.* "Disgruntled." *Click.* Mia lowered the camera. "I can't tell if you're trying to smile or if that's your disgruntled face."

"It's probably just his face." Einstein appeared from the back of the tent, one hand pressed to his forehead. "Those stupid poles are broken. I swear they don't fit. Did you get any good ones?" He pointed at the camera in Mia's hands.

Mia shrugged. "I don't know. Homer wasn't very responsive and there's no preview on these." She shook the camera and then studied the back as though she expected a picture to appear like the answer dice floating to the surface of a Magic 8 Ball.

"So," Einstein said slowly, "you're not even sure that those things work?"

"Nope." Mia pointed the camera at Einstein's face and clicked.

"And you're taking pictures anyway?"

"Yup."

"That's stupid."

"Steiner," Homer said, shaking his way loose from the tent door's netting. "S.F., dude."

"It's not stupid," Mia said. She held the camera in front of her and tilted it toward her stomach. "Baby's first picture." *Click. Click. Click.* "It's an act of faith." She slid the camera into the old hiking backpack D.B. had given her. "Most things are."

Einstein and Mia probably could have gone back and forth all night, but a new voice entered the dusk.

"Hey there. I saw your headlights from 'cross the way." The girl who appeared from the edge of the clearing had a voice like a heavy whisper, a combination of syrup and concrete. She had dark skin, a broad nose, and wide-set eyes framed by thick eyebrows above and shadows underneath.

Mia was the first one to respond. "Hello. I'm Mia." She pointed over her left shoulder. "These guys are Homer and Einstein. They're brothers. Homer's tall and very sweet and Einstein's a genius. We're just camping out for the night."

The girl glanced at the tent. It looked like a candle that had melted on one side. "I see that. Usually, tourists stay at the new hotels on Route 17. It gets real muggy in the woods, even in December."

"You live here?" Einstein asked.

"Back yonder." She pointed vaguely in the direction she'd come from. "I like the trees. Plus, it's quieter—or least it's quieter than the new part of town."

"It's crazyville over there," Mia said, rolling her fingers over her stomach like it was a drum. "There's all those empty buildings and then the line of people and the movie folks with fancy-pants equipment and lots of cigarettes."

"Actually, they're TV people. They shoot the show."

"What show?"

"*American Oracle*. On every Monday. Prime time." Even though the daylight had faded to the point where shadows were starting to disappear, the girl must have been able to see Mia's, Homer's, and Einstein's puzzled expressions, because she added, "Prime time's between eight and eleven p.m." She looked at each of them in turn, settling on Mia, who shrugged apologetically. "Huh, y'all really don't know who I am, do ya?"

Homer studied her face. It could be familiar, but it was hard to tell. She had on thick makeup, and her loose, billowing clothing was the same style as the one that hundreds of women who stepped into La Isla Souvenirs had been wearing that year. "Sorry," he finally said. "I don't think we do. But," he added, not wanting to be rude, "we're not from around here."

"Well, that shouldn't matter. *American Oracle*'s on network

TV. But let's start at how-ya-do. My name's Daphne Treme. I'm the Oracle of Pythia Springs."

Homer nudged a tent-pole clip with his sneaker. "You tell people their futures? Like a psychic?"

Daphne shook her head. "It's more complicated than that. But not so complicated that it doesn't work for TV. Hey, I've got an early day tomorrow. We start shooting *American Oracle* during the ten a.m. session. Y'all should come watch. In fact"— she glanced at Homer and Einstein's half-erected tent—"why don't y'all come crash in my trailer. December in Pythia doesn't get too bad, but the weather's mighty unpredictable. It can get down to the thirties some nights."

"We wouldn't want to—" Homer started to say, but Mia interrupted.

"That'd be super. Mr. and Mrs. Jackson had a double-wide and it was so cozy." Mia scooped her bag off the ground and fell in beside Daphne. "We had eight of us in there, but it wasn't bad."

"Who are Mr. and Mrs. Jackson?" Homer said as he bent into the half-raised tent and swept the stuff that had fallen out of his bag into a pile.

"She didn't hear you." Einstein's sneakers appeared in Homer's peripheral vision. "They already started walking."

"Oh." Homer shoved everything into his duffel, zipped the tent door closed, and stood up. "This is a little weird, right? We should get Mia and set—" Homer felt more than heard the back of the tent, the one part he and Einstein had actually gotten to stand up, billow to the ground. "Shit."

"Set up the tents?" said Einstein, gently kicking a pole. "I think at this point we'd have to enlist NASA to make that happen."

Homer glanced at the pile of faded canvas. "Yeah, you're probably right." He flung the duffel over his shoulder. "Let's catch up."

THE PARABLE OF THE ACCIDENTAL ORACLE AND THE FORGOTTEN PLACE

THE STORY OF THE FORGOTTEN Place is not so different from the stories of many other disremembered locales. Once, the town had been prosperous; then Company X, Y, or Z had pulled up stakes, jumped ship, skedaddled, boarded the proverbial last train out, leaving a community to remake itself out of dust and ruins.

Before it was the Forgotten Place, the secluded town in the hills of South Carolina had been a harmonious world unto itself. It had buildings painted the colors of Easter eggs, and mail carriers who smiled and always had dog biscuits in their pockets. Neighbors kept their doors open after dusk, and every Sunday the Divine Promise Baptist Choir sang gospel so powerful the walls of the church were permanently curved.

Unfortunately, by time the Accidental Oracle was born, that town was all but gone.

The Accidental Oracle got out as soon as she turned eighteen:

two days after her high school graduation. She let folks believe she was moving on to find fame and fortune in the Big-Wide-Elsewhere. She figured there was no need to upset anyone with the full truth: she was leaving to escape just as much as she was to succeed.

Everyone said she was going to make it. Her theater teacher raved about her "God-given talent." Her mama told her that if her name wasn't on the marquees of the best theaters within a year, then the sky was purple and up was down.

They were right.

And they were wrong.

It turns out that trying to find your place in the Big-Wide-Elsewhere is really hard. Mostly because there are so many others trying to do the same.

The Accidental Oracle was just another smart, lovely, talented girl in a city full of smart, lovely, talented young people—all of them determined never to return to their own versions of the Forgotten Place.

She fought the good fight for nearly four years. She waited tables at night and went to auditions during the day. She lived in a crowded apartment ten blocks from the subway station at the very end of the line to save money for a voice coach, acting coach, style coach. She worked and worked and worked until the Tuesday morning she woke up and realized she was too tired to keep running in sand. That morning, she called the manager at the uptown restaurant where she was scheduled for the dinner shift and explained that she wouldn't be in at four o'clock, or ever again, for that matter. She left a month's rent and the few pieces of furniture she'd accumulated in her shoddy apartment and boarded a bus that dropped her off two towns over from the Forgotten Place.

Back in her grandma's house for the first time since she turned eighteen, the Accidental Oracle slept for days. Then she got restless and started walking.

She found the crack in the earth beneath the sycamore at the edge of the clearing by happenstance. Hundreds of times before, she had walked through the field where the Company X factory had once stood. But on the day that changed her life, she was feeling particularly exhausted and heavy footed. Indeed, if she hadn't caught the toe of her sneaker on one of the sycamore's gnarled roots, she never would have lain stunned on the ground at the base of the tree's massive trunk and breathed in the strange fumes drifting out of a crack in the earth like smoke from a freshly lit cigarette. The fumes and the fall made her feel foggy headed and then remarkably clear and desperate to talk. She was still babbling hours later when she stumbled back to her *ya-ya*'s home.

That night, she saw things: the numbers for a two-thousand-dollar scratch ticket; her cousin breaking his toe; her mama full of regret after cutting her bangs. The next morning, the

Accidental Oracle noticed three new scars on the back of her right hand. At first, she thought they were from the fall. With time, she would learn otherwise.

Within weeks, news of the Accidental Oracle's abilities began drawing strangers into town—including a Hollywood executive producer, who saw that the Accidental Oracle had everything prime-time America loved: beauty, mystery, and a rags-to-riches fairy tale that so many still needed to believe in.

After *American Oracle* went on the air, folks from the four corners of the world began traveling to the Forgotten Place. Some came thousands of miles just to call the Accidental Oracle a devil worshipper, a sorceress, a sinner. But believers came from all over, too. They arrived with hope in their eyes and unanswered prayers on their lips. They called her an angel, a messenger, a miracle.

The trouble with your life being a miracle is that people expect miracles of you.

Some pilgrims left the Forgotten Place that had become a Somewhere Place furious, heartsick, and frustrated by their inability to make sense of the garbled words that fell out of the Accidental Oracle's mouth. But many more (it seemed) drove away crying grateful tears and marveling at the lightness of their newly unburdened hearts.

Every time the Accidental Oracle visited the crack at the base of the gnarled sycamore, it cost her a piece of herself. She met each dawn with fresh marks on her skin and an ache in her bones that only patience and daylight could warm away. Her grandma begged her to stop, but she refused. She had stumbled upon a gift, and it had given her everything she thought she wanted.

THE STRANGEST SHOW ON EARTH

IT TOOK HOMER LONGER THAN it should have to remember where he was when he woke up. He spent a solid minute staring at the ceiling tiles and wondering why he wasn't looking at the glow-in-the-dark stars his dads had decorated his bedroom with when he was ten. Only once he stood up did he feel oriented.

Daphne's trailer was neat and cozy and the air mattress he'd shared with Einstein was a million times more comfortable than the slabs-of-concrete beds at La Mancha Magnífico Motel. But Homer still felt like he hadn't slept at all. And it wasn't just because Einstein was a kicker and a blanket stealer or that Mia, who had refused Daphne's offer to take the bed, had slept on the couch and been talking in her sleep for the better part of the night. It was something he couldn't place. He was worried and he didn't know why.

Homer stretched his arms above his head and then followed

the smell of coffee to the small kitchen. He had to rub his eyes twice before he could make out the note Daphne had stuck to the front of the coffeemaker: "Help yourself! Milk's in the fridge. Sugar to the left of the sink."

When Homer stepped out of the trailer, he didn't notice the cold right away. The steam rising off his coffee blended with the thick fog, and it took a few yards before the December air started to siphon the warmth of sleep from his skin.

He had just taken his first sip—gulp, really—when he saw Daphne perched on a rock near the periphery of the yard. Her back was as straight as the tree trunks in the woods behind her. The mug that she clutched to her chest was, like Homer's, releasing whispers of steam. Her face was angled toward the ground, her long neck exposed to the outstretched shadows of tree limbs.

Daphne was so still and looked so deep in thought that Homer didn't want to disturb her. Unfortunately, two steps into going the opposite direction, one of his huge feet landed on a twig, snapping it in two and making a sound like shotgun going off.

Damn.

"You're up early." When Daphne spoke, she didn't lift her head. She kept gazing down. At what exactly, Homer couldn't tell. *She's a psychic*, he thought. *Maybe it's something only she can see.*

"Sorry. I didn't know you were out here. I can—"

Daphne gestured for Homer to come closer. "It's warmer in the sun. It'll get better by morning-session time, even in the shade. Don't worry."

Daphne was wearing cut-off shorts, a too-large flannel, and no shoes. As Homer stepped closer, he saw something he hadn't noticed last night when Daphne had on pants and long sleeves: her legs, feet, hands, and wrists were marked with lines of various lengths and in various stages of healing. They looked painful, and they reminded Homer of the time he'd cut his thumb on a steak knife when he was little. D.B had panicked. Christian had been calm, and Homer had been excited to get stitches. With the memory, Homer felt an ache in his chest. This was only the third day of the trip, but his dads, and the island, already seemed thousands of miles away.

Homer didn't realize he was staring at Daphne until her dark eyes caught his.

"I used to be prettier."

"Sorry. I didn't mean to stare."

"No 'sorry' needed. I'm used to it. They don't hurt. The scars." Daphne held a hand in front of her face like she was trying to decide whether or not she liked a ring. "The other stuff? That hurts. The cuts just prickle. They freak people out, though. That's why I cover up most of the time." She grasped her mug with two hands again, wiggling her fingers until they overlapped. "My agent says wearing gloves gives me a mystique. But when I'm out here, I like to feel the air." She shifted a little higher on the rock. "I've always liked the cold. That's part of the reason why I left Pythia in the first place. Gets too hot in here."

"I'm not freaked out. Sorry. I mean. I feel like I've interrupted something." There was nothing accusatory in Daphne's tone or her eyes, but Homer felt embarrassed anyway.

"You say 'sorry' way too much for such a nice guy."

"You're not the first person to tell me that."

"I know."

The way she said those two words, "I know," made Homer wonder what else she knew about him. He didn't believe in psychics, astrology, or any of that kooky stuff. But when he'd finally fallen asleep the night before, Daphne and Mia had still been up and whispering across the small card table in the kitchen. *Has Mia been talking about me?* He cleared his throat and asked a question out loud instead. "So, why'd you come back to Pythia?"

"Couldn't make it in the big city." Daphne poured what was left of her coffee out. The ground steamed where the hot liquid met the pine needles and dirt. "I wanted to be an actress. Problem is, I wasn't any good." She snorted, then slid off the boulder. "Me and every other twenty-something girl looking to escape a trash heap town. All of us discovering the hard way that a pretty face and a great ass don't make you special out there." She nodded toward the woods.

Homer wasn't sure if she expected a response, but he gave

one anyway. "At least you figured out what you believed in and went for it. Lots of people don't get that far." He ground a rock into the soft dirt with his foot. "Seems like you're doing great here. Your own reality show. That's got to be cool." A gust breaking through the trees passed over the top of Homer's head like a cold invisible hand, making him shiver.

"It's something." Daphne wrapped her arms around her ribs, letting her empty mug dangle from her fingertips. "And I've got time to figure out what I want to do next. 'Stead of living on the fumes of yesterday's dreams." Her words were heavy, but they hung in the air for several stretched-out moments before her tone changed completely. "I better go get ready. More coffee?" She jiggled her mug.

"No. No, thanks. I'm good. Thank you, though." When Homer shook his mug in return, coffee sloshed over the sides.

Daphne's laugh cut through the morning's stillness like a plane through clouds. "I'll make another pot just in case." Still smiling, she turned and walked across the clearing toward the trailer.

Homer heard Mia singing and the sound of water running through pipes coming from one of the trailer windows.

> *"For one more night I'm in your heart. Oh. Oh. Oh.*
> *Da. Da. Whole of mine. Whoopsie. Awaaaaaaaaay.*
> *Something. Something . . . duh da duh . . . here and now.*
> *Yeah. Yeah. Yeah. Last song of our lives."*

"Hey, Daphne," Homer called.

She kept one hand on the trailer's railing when she turned. "Yeah?"

"Thank you. For this." Homer held up his mug, careful this time not to move too quickly. "For, uh, all of it." What he'd been planning to say had been much more eloquent, at least it had been in his head.

"Most folks ask a lot more of me than this," Daphne said. "But—" Her smile faded, her expression becoming as unreadable as the ink words in a rain-soaked notebook. "You're welcome. I'm grateful for the company."

This time, Homer knew he wasn't expected to respond.

Daphne really seemed to mean it when she said Einstein was "just a peach." And if she was sick of his going on and on about the looming apocalypse, nothing in her demeanor suggested it.

In fact, as they moved closer and closer to the clearing where she performed her show, Daphne's questions came quicker and quicker even as her steps slowed:

"What's an existential risk?"

"Why would super-fast atoms make a black hole?"

"Do you suppose the scientists get depressed, thinking about the end of the world all the time?"

As socially inept as his brother could be, Homer knew his ramblings weren't always annoying. Sometimes, it was even kind of nice to let Einstein talk at you. Not because what he was saying was interesting, or even understandable, but because Einstein was so unapologetically enthusiastic. He didn't care that the things he thought were cool actually weren't. He saw mysteries to solve, and that was all he needed.

When Daphne and Einstein reached the line where the dirt of the forest path gave way to flattened grass, Daphne halted like she'd hit an invisible wall. Einstein went a few steps into the clearing before he realized she was no longer beside him, and then he doubled back. In the time it took Homer and Mia to catch up, something in the air changed. It felt charged. Bizarre. As though someone somewhere had connected a plug that had never been connected before and switched on the atmosphere.

Homer and Mia stopped beside Daphne. She was clutching the sides of her dress like it was the only thing holding her to the ground. The buzzing sound that Homer had started hearing just minutes after they'd left Daphne's trailer, the sound he'd assumed was coming from clouds of insects hidden by the trees, was, in fact, the combined whisperings of an expectant crowd.

Mia and Einstein shuffled toward each other, standing shoulder to shoulder, forming a barrier between Daphne and the hundreds of people sitting in tidy rows—waiting to see her: the American Oracle.

"It feels like someone lowered a glass dome over this place," Einstein whispered, "and then stripped all the atoms inside of their electrons."

"I don't know what that means," Mia whispered back. "But if you just said this is weird, then I agree."

"This is nothing," Daphne said, bending down to run her hand over a patch of grass still glazed with frost. "Just wait until the asking starts." She pressed her hand, red from the cold, to one cheek, then the other. "They all come for different reasons. They all want the same thing." The water on her cheeks glistened like tears. "Least that's what my *ya-ya* says."

Homer glanced at Daphne's profile. The heavy makeup, fake eyelashes, and gauzy dress made her nearly unrecognizable as the girl in flannel and bare feet he'd been talking to fewer than two hours earlier. He had to clear his throat before speaking. "What do they want? The people, I mean." He nodded toward the waiting crowd.

"A performance." Daphne sighed. "I get the nerves before every show. Gotta shake it off." She closed her eyes and wiggled from side to side. "O-kay." Daphne opened her eyes. "I'll see y'all after." Her transformation from world-weary to world famous was as sudden and blinding as the sun breaking through clouds.

"She said she wasn't any good as an actress," Homer whispered as they made their way to the last row of benches.

The worry in Homer's thoughts must have seeped into his voice, because Mia sat down beside him—her right shoulder pressed so close to his left that he could smell Daphne's shampoo in her hair—and reached for his hand, lacing her fingers with his one by one.

Mia's grip was warm and soft, and Homer's brain felt even more jumbled than before. Still, he was grateful that she didn't let go.

When a tall man in a black suit and shiny shoes stepped onto a wooden platform set under a drooping sycamore tree, the crowd hushed. The man kept his smile wide as he dragged a microphone stand to the center of the makeshift stage.

"Ladies and gentlemen. I'm Gerard Smith, your host. Miss Clara Belle, who will be joining the Oracle onstage, is my assistant." Gerard's rich voice filled the clearing, pressed against the trees. "Welcome to Pythia Springs."

The crowd clapped politely.

"You're here because you have questions." Gerard paused to smile at a guy in slouchy black jeans standing just to the side of the first row of benches and holding a huge video camera. "Today's the day you get answers. But first, a few housekeeping items." He clapped his hands. "Please turn off your cell phones. No pictures. No filming—except, of course, for the crew from the number-three reality TV show on CGH Family, *American Oracle*." Gerard gestured to the sides of the platform, where more guys dressed in black were fiddling with cameras on tripods. "Participants will be chosen at random. Unfortunately, the Oracle will not give *everyone* a reading, but we promise that even if you don't Get. To. Ask. That. Ques-chin. Burn-ing. Inside. Your. Soul"—Gerard let each word ripple over the heads of the crowd—"you'll leave here forever changed by what you've seen."

Einstein leaned over Mia and whispered out of the side of his mouth, "Really? This is the biggest bunch—"

Homer didn't hear the rest.

"Without further ado," Gerard said, "I give you Daphne Treme, the American Oracle."

When he dropped his arms, there was a boom like a frozen tree limb cracking, followed by a cloud of thick smoke that covered the stage.

"Over the top much?" This time Einstein didn't bother to whisper. The big man in a polo shirt sitting to Einstein's right shook his head disapprovingly.

The smoke cleared quickly, revealing Daphne sitting in a throne-like armchair at the center of the platform. A woman in a very tight red dress and high heels was perched on a stool to Daphne's right. This time, the crowd's clapping was certain, strong, more like the applause of fans in a sports stadium than the palm patting of churchgoers in pews. The woman in heels—Homer assumed she was Clara Belle—nodded at Gerard, who gestured for a cameraman to follow him. With that, the show began.

The first person Gerard handed the microphone to reminded Homer of the old man who owned the bed and breakfast at the far end of the Los Plátanos boardwalk. His left shoulder dipped lower than his right, and the hand that grasped the mike shook from age or nerves or a combination of the two. The tremor in his voice made his question that much sadder. He wanted to know if his wife had made it to heaven.

Daphne's tangled response didn't make any sense—at least not to Homer.

"She's found a paradise of her own creation, one spun with sugar and cinnamon. She says the creek is full, the sun doesn't dip into the horizon, and it's always morning and never too late."

The old man bowed his head, and though Homer couldn't see his face, he noticed that the man's back looked a little straighter as he sat down.

All the answers that followed were just as odd and dis-combobulated as the first. And yet the askers, no matter how desperate the question, all seemed to understand, to hear something in the gibberish that was as clear as to them as the words of a neon sign set against the otherwise empty dark.

There will come a time when yellow will be the right color to hear. You'll know where.

The past has not happened. Not yet. It will. But false hope won't make it the same as it was before.

Be generous with your weaknesses. Wishing alone won't make the pumpkin into a pine tree.

To a stocky man in a fleece pullover who asked about his estranged daughter, Daphne said, "She's made a beautiful life out of dust and tumbleweeds. She's pulled the moon closer with her truthful smile. When you send the letter, add a flower. She'll open it this time." The man nodded and wiped his eyes on his sleeve as he handed the mike back to Gerard.

The guy who spoke next grabbed the microphone before Gerard had the chance to pose for the camera crew. "Yeah. I've got more of a statement than a question." Maybe it was the way the upturned collar on his trench coat hid his face or maybe Gerard didn't like how the guy was shifting from side to side like a boxer about to throw a punch. Whatever his reasons, Gerard raised his hand and two wide men in black overcoats and headsets appeared next to him.

"I—" The man in the trench coat hesitated, glanced at Gerard and the men with headsets, and then spoke so quickly everything he said sounded like one big word. "Whatyou'redoing hereisthedevil'sworkandtheOneabovewillpunishyouinhellever-lastingforyoursins." His rant done, the man dropped the mike to the ground, held his hands in the air, and started walking across the clearing toward a break in the woods. The men with headsets followed a yard or so behind.

Gerard picked up the microphone and plastered a big smile on his face. "Whew. I apologize for that ugly interruption. Okay, who's next?"

With each question, Daphne slumped a little bit more. Each answer she gave transformed into a hand pressing against the back of her neck. When a woman with a cane pushed herself to her feet, the microphone grasped in her free hand, her mouth opening to ask her sad or anxious or pained question, Daphne folded in half like an antique doll and didn't sit back up.

Just like that, the strange show was over.

It was horrifying, how well rehearsed everything was that happened next. Gerard excused the crowd, explaining that the Oracle was done for the day and the gift shop was open until five as Clara Belle waved and the two security guys reappeared to carry Daphne off the platform.

Watching this, Homer felt like Einstein's glass dome had actually been lowered over the clearing and he needed to escape immediately, but Mia's hand, still gripping his, held him in place as he started to stand.

"Let the rest of them go. Then we'll find her," she said.

Einstein nodded in agreement, so Homer stayed put and they waited until they were the only ones left, save for two men in coveralls who came to sweep up the tissues and tickets left behind on the flattened grass.

When they got back to Daphne's trailer, there was a small fleet of cars parked out front, including the TV crew's huge SUV.

The elderly woman who answered the door might have looked sweet under other circumstances. Her hair was neatly pinned like a movie star from the 1930s, her swishy dress a comforting shade of sky blue. But at that moment, she looked like a woman who was expecting—and ready for—a fight.

"Yes?"

"Uh, hi." Einstein's hand was still raised from knocking. He lowered it quickly. "We . . . we wanted to check on Daphne."

"We're her friends," Mia added.

The woman looked them up and down, head to toe, one by one. "How do you know my granddaughter?"

"She let us—"

"She helped us last night," Homer interrupted Einstein. He suspected that Daphne's grandmother wouldn't like the fact that her granddaughter had let three tourists sleep in her trailer home.

The woman eased her grip on the door handle, but her expression remained guarded. "You'll have to come back another time. She overdid it again and needs to rest. I was just kicking those fool TV people out before y'all arrived." She started to shut the door, but Mia's voice stopped her.

"Does it happen a lot? Her collapsing?"

Daphne's grandmother made her free hand into a fist, squeezed it tight, then looked up. "Let me tell you something. When that baby of yours comes into the world, you're gonna want to make it so that little soul never feels even a thimbleful of pain." The hardness in her voice dissolved like a sugar cube in hot water. "And it will break your heart when that child goes invitin' all that bad stuff into her life after you spent most of yours trying to keep those hurts away."

Einstein tucked his nose into his sweatshirt. Homer looked at his feet. Only Mia seemed to know what to say.

"I'm sorry."

"Oh, child." Daphne's grandmother was weary, strong, and kind all at once. "It's not your fault. And Lord knows, I shouldn't make a mama-to-be worry. I beg Him for guidance, but Daphne's like her father, stubborn and hungry for bigger things." She shook her head gently. "She tells me, 'Ya-Ya, open your Bible—all those heroes and saints, they had to suffer some to do good.' She says, 'Ya-Ya, we all make sacrifices—at least I know I'm making mine.' I suppose she's not too far from the truth." Daphne's grandmother tapped her fingertips against the door, each tiny *ping* a period at the end of whatever silent prayers she was reciting in her head.

Homer found his voice. "I'm sorry we've upset you. We wanted to make sure Daphne—"

"I should go check on her. I don't trust those TV folks any farther than I can throw 'em. I'll tell her y'all came by. 'Kay?"

"Thank you."

Daphne's grandmother nodded and started to shut the door, but stopped abruptly. "You're Homer?"

"Yes. That's me."

"I'm feeling my age today. Forgettin' everything." She fished a folded piece of paper out of her front pocket. "Daphne said to give you this. Said to tell you it was the first one she saw."

"I—"

"Hope it didn't cost her something?"

Homer nodded, closing his hands around the paper scrap.

"It did. But you can't blame yourself for that." Daphne's grandmother smiled sadly and pushed the door the rest of the way shut.

★ ★ ★

Homer waited until they were back at the car to open Daphne's note and read it out loud. "If you believe in gravity, you already believe in something higher than yourself."

"Huh," Mia said as she put her bag in the Banana's trunk. "What do you think it means?"

"From a physicist's point of view," Einstein, who was half hidden behind a pine tree, shouted, "it doesn't make sense at all."

Mia looked around the trunk lid at Homer. "What do you think?"

Homer hesitated before answering. "I don't know." But he did. He just didn't know how to explain.

THE ROAD TO AWAY / THE ROAD TO SOMEWHERE

IT TOOK MILES AND MILES of pavement between them and Pythia Springs for Homer to ease his grip on the steering wheel.

Mia and Einstein had switched spots, so now she was curled across the backseat, her arms folded for a pillow, and Einstein was slumped against the passenger-seat window up front. Homer couldn't make himself get back on the highway. If that meant he had to drive longer to make up the time, it was worth it not to be surrounded by tractor trailers and trucks with overstuffed beds. And he needed to let them sleep: Mia and Einstein both. When he slowed to a stop at the first real traffic light he'd seen for hours, Homer glanced to his right. Einstein's head was thrown back and his mouth was slightly open. Homer reached over and slid the glasses off his brother's face and set them in a cup holder.

"Don't be worried about Daphne. She'll be okay." Mia's voice was barely louder than a whisper. "She's very smart."

"I'm not worried." Homer glanced in the rearview mirror. Mia was still resting her head on her arms, but her eyes were open, and they met his in the mirror.

"You're a rotten liar, Homer."

Homer thought about protesting, but only for half a heartbeat. "Yeah, I know. It's on the list."

"List?"

"Of things I'm bad at. Lying falls somewhere in between juggling and biology."

"You're silly, Homer. You're great at tons of stuff." Mia's pitch rose as she continued. "You're nice and sweet and tall and good at picking up heavy things. And everyone likes you because you smile with your whole face, not just your mouth."

Homer pretended to search for a radio station so he wouldn't be tempted to look over his shoulder. Most of the time it was okay that Mia didn't like him more than as a friend, but sometimes, when she said stuff like that, a dam inside him threatened to crumble, to flood his chest with a feeling that wasn't quite sadness but wasn't quite regret either. It was like experiencing a memory in the present. It took the Banana drifting onto the rumble strip for Homer to snap out of his thoughts.

"Question. What's the worst thing you've ever done?" Mia asked.

"What do you mean?"

"Like, have you robbed a bank?"

"Nope." Homer put on his blinker and passed the minivan

he'd been stuck behind for over an hour. He'd had plenty of time to assemble an image of the family inside from the many stickers lining the van's rusted bumper: the parents were proud of their honor students, wanted peace for the world and Mick Swanzy for Sheriff, and they loved their dachshund—a lot.

"Have you ever kidnapped anyone?"

"Nope." Homer felt the corners of his mouth twitch. He could hear the smile in Mia's voice, and that made it nearly impossible not to smile with her.

"Masterminded the takeover of a politically unstable country?"

"Ha. You've been spending too much time with Einstein."

The backseat crackled as Mia shifted around. "So spill. What's the worst thing you've ever done?"

Homer slid his hands up and down the steering wheel. The view outside had morphed from dense South Carolina woods into never-ending North Carolina fields, scrubby, but still tinted with green even in December. "My dads love to bring up the time I set one of their tea towels on fire in the backyard."

"What's a tea towel?"

"It's a useless piece of fabric that just takes space away from towels that are actually useful."

"Oh." Mia frowned. "Is that why you set it on fire? Because you were mad at it?"

"No." Homer coughed. "It was an accident. I was trying to do a voodoo ceremony and—"

"Why? Were you making a voodoo doll of someone?"

"No. My dads said that I had a stage where I was super into rituals. D.B. was worried I was going to join a cult, but Christian said I was 'emotionally mature' and should be 'encouraged to explore' my 'innate spiritual nature.'" Homer laughed. "Or something like that. Then he went to the hardware store and bought me a bunch of battery-powered candles and hid all the matches."

"Huh." Mia sat up. Out of the corner of his eye, Homer saw her wrap her arms around her stomach. "You're lucky," Mia said quietly. She turned toward a side window. "That Christian and D.B. found you. Got you."

"Yeah. I know." Part of him wanted to shout and pound his fists against the steering wheel. Yeah, he was lucky, and yeah, it really sucked that Mia wasn't. It sucked that she never got a new family. Another part of him wanted to stop the car, pull Mia into a hug, and tell her she was amazing. That any family would have been incredibly lucky to have her. That he was pretty sure, very sure, that he was in love with her. Instead he kept his hands on the wheel, cleared his throat, and hoped that words that made sense would come out of his mouth. "I was a strange little kid." Homer shook his head. "I guess I still am. Strange, that is."

"I used to make my stuffed animals pray when I was in fourth grade. Every night before bed, I'd line up Elly Pants, Boo Bear, and Mike."

"Mike?"

"Mike the Giraffe. I was still living with my bio mom then, but it was around the time her drinking got so, so bad. She yelled a lot. Fought with her boyfriend. I started going to my room earlier and earlier every night, you know, to get out of the way. But I wasn't tired enough to fall asleep, so I'd set my toys up and pretend they were praying." Mia laughed. "I didn't know any real prayers, so I had them recite Christmas carols and then ask God for the stuff I secretly wanted."

"Let me guess. Mike the Giraffe's favorite was 'The Twelve Days of Christmas'?"

"Because of all the animals?" Mia said, reaching down to the floor. When she sat up, she had a pen woven between her fingers.

"Yup."

"Ha." Mia put one end of the pen in her mouth. "You're so clever, Homer."

"No, I'm not. Glad you're fooled, though." Homer felt his cheeks flush. "I'm also not a germ-o-phobe or anything, but it might not be a good idea to put that pen in your mouth."

"This pen? Why?" Mia kept chewing.

"Because it was on the floor and I don't think the Banana's previous owner was concerned about the mats staying clean."

"Huh." Mia chomped down twice more before spitting the pen cap into her palm. "Good point." She dropped the cap and pen on top of a stack of magazines at her feet.

"So, what'd the stuffed animals ask for?"

"Oh, stupid stuff." Mia made a dismissive motion with her hand.

Homer decided not to press her, but he couldn't keep himself from asking one more question. "What's the worst thing *you've* done?"

"Ever?"

"Yup."

"I stole something."

"A big something?"

"Yeah. The first time I got to go back and live with my mom, I stole her car keys."

"Where did you want to go?"

"Oh, no. I didn't want to drive. I was only fourteen. I did it because I didn't want my mom to drive. I don't remember how long it was before she started drinking again, but one night she was loopy and I took her car keys. Whew. She got so, so mad."

"You were trying to help her," Homer said lamely.

"Yeah. But then I told Ms. Kincaid, the social worker, about hiding the keys. I thought she'd be happy that my mom couldn't drive, but instead my mom got in trouble and Ms. Kincaid said I had to live somewhere else again." Mia stretched her arms above her head, her mouth open in a wide yawn. "Awww, why am I such a sleepyhead today?"

"You should sleep. It's been a crazy twenty-four hours." Homer looked at the map on his phone. "Besides, we've got lots of time before we reach anywhere that might have a hotel."

"You sure?"

"Yeah. I like taking the smaller roads. It'll make the trip longer, but it's much more interesting than the highway." What Homer didn't say was that he was happy to draw out the time he had left with Mia for as long as he possibly could.

The old leather of the backseat crackled as Mia curled up. This time her face was turned away from Homer and she pressed her arms close to her chest instead of folding them beneath her head.

"Uh, Mia?"

"Yeah?" Mia said, tucking her knees up higher.

"I'm sorry. About your mom. It sucks." Homer glanced in the rearview mirror. Saw Mia's shoulders rise and fall, and then looked back at the road. *Maybe she's already asleep.*

When she did speak, Homer could only hear some of what she said.

"Others have . . . worse. I was . . . because . . ."

Homer didn't say anything else after that. And when Einstein woke up, he let him pick where they'd stay that night.

THE VISION OF
A FAILED UTOPIA

"**HOMES, IF I HOLD IT** much longer, I'll increase my chances of developing cystitis, which also puts me at risk for permanent damage to the kidneys and other internal organs."

"Cist— What?" Homer looked down at the directions he'd printed at the Hideaway Motel's business center that morning. He'd been in a rush and yanked the paper out of the printer before the ink had had a chance to set, and so he was left with smudged directions to the one college he'd promised D.B. he'd visit.

"Cystitis. It's the medical term for bladder inflammation."

"Steiner, if you see a place, we'll stop. But given that we've passed nothing but horses and farmhouses since we got off the highway, you'll probably have to hold it until we get to Pillar College. Or you can water a tree."

Homer glanced in the rearview mirror. Einstein's cheeks were puffed out and he was squirming from side to side.

"You look like a blowfish right now," he said, turning his eyes back to the two-lane country road. "At risk for cystitis? How do you come up with this stuff?"

"Really?" Einstein went from blowfish to puzzled, his head tilted in a way that suggested he didn't know whether Homer was kidding or not.

"Yes, really."

"I'm a genius."

Einstein, Homer noticed, said "I'm a genius" the way another person might say "I'm six feet tall" or "I'm an enthusiastic fisherman."

"What do you guys think about 'Oscar'?" Mia had found a pair of sunglasses with plastic pineapples on the sides under the bed in her motel room that morning and hadn't taken them off since. Homer couldn't look at her without smiling. "Or 'Penelope'? I could use 'Penny' for short. 'Lucky Penny,' that's a cute nickname, don't you think?"

"Name for what?" Einstein hollered from the backseat.

"For Tadpole, silly," Mia said, shaking a paperback book in the space between the front seats. "I need a real name. Look what I found at the gas station while you guys were getting doughnuts."

"One Thousand and One Names for Your Baby," Einstein read. "If there're one thousand and one names in there, I think you can find something better than 'Oscar.'"

"Steiner, S.F.," Homer said without much conviction. He

was too busy trying to keep the Banana on the road while figuring out if he should be looking for Silver Pond Road or Slither Pond Road to put much energy into calling his little brother on his rudeness.

"No way that's an S.F. Mia asked for my opinion, right?"

Homer saw Mia nod and wiggle back and forth as she turned the pages of her book. "Yup. Yup. I asked. Can't get mad at the answer. What about 'Ernest'? Or 'Anastasia'?" She pushed the pineapple sunglasses back up her nose and tucked her candy-apple-red hair behind her ears.

That simple gesture, how Mia brushed her hair off her face, was so effortlessly hot that Homer had to force himself to look away.

"Now that I think about it," she continued, "I should probably go, too. Bladder infection? No, thank you."

"Really? Again?" Homer asked.

"Preggo ladies have to pee all the time," Mia said as she reached down and shuffled the magazines at her feet until she found a particularly thick one. She set it on her lap. "According to Dr. Traynor—" Mia cleared her throat and, in an exaggerated accent somewhere between British and Australian, read, "During your pregnancy the amount of blood in your body increases by almost fifty percent— Wait, that wasn't the part I wanted." She began flipping through the pages. "I'll find the part about needing to go all the time. Just give me a sec."

"They have a magazine just for pregnant ladies?" Einstein

asked, peering through the crack between Mia's seat and the door.

"Nope." Mia looked up. "It's a parenting magazine. Homer got it for me when I found out I'd be having a Tadpole."

"He did?" Einstein replied. "Isn't that something the baby's dad should—"

"Look, I can't read the printout and my cell doesn't get reception." Homer said, dropping his phone in one of the Banana's giant cup holders. "There's a farm stand ahead. You guys can pee. I can get directions. Win. Win. Win."

Mia clapped her hands together. "I hope they have pickled beets."

"Pickled beets?" Homer asked.

Out of the corner of his eye, he saw Mia shrug. "Babies crave strange things, Homer. What can I tell you?"

"Guess I learned something today," Homer said, taking a left turn at the sign for Doxy Community Farm Stand into a dirt parking lot.

"Oh, that's nothing. Did you know that babies don't have kneecaps and they can't swallow and breathe at the same time for months and months? Plus . . ." Mia, still wearing her ridiculous sunglasses, continued talking as she slid out of the Banana and walked toward a red, shacklike structure with a hand-painted sign proudly declaring "Open All Year!!!" above the door. She was already inside by the time Homer and Einstein caught up.

"Huh," Einstein said, scanning the dusky space. "I've never

been to a farm stand, but aren't they supposed to have . . . stuff? Farm stuff?"

The store was nearly empty save for a few jars of jam on a counter above an old-fashioned metal cash register and a handful of sad-looking potatoes in a bin close to the door.

"Maybe they're closed," Homer replied, swatting at the strings of cobweb he'd walked right into off his face. "You might need to water a tree after all, Steiner."

"Nuh-uh." Einstein shook his head and hopped from one foot to the other. "I'm still itchy from the bites I got yesterday—in places you can't scratch in public."

"Hello?" Mia called, pushing her sunglasses on top of her head as she stepped away from the lonely potatoes and farther into the shack.

"Hello! Are you here for the tour?" A voice, high-pitched with enthusiasm, bounced around the empty space. "Brother Bob is going to be so excited." The tall man who strode into the shack through a door in the back right corner was dressed in denim overalls dotted with multiple patches, each a different color and pattern. His stained shirt had uneven sleeves, and his floppy straw hat was at least two sizes too big. "Bob, get out here! You have some folks here for the tour."

"What tour?" Homer asked, but if the oddly dressed man heard him, he gave no indication.

"Okay." The man clapped his bony hands together, then ran his long fingers through his stringy beard as if he were thinking deeply. "What can I tell you about our community? Let's see, we're a farming collective, in the spirit of Jeremiah Johacksenburg's grand vision. We like to call him J.J. around here." The man guffawed and slapped a hand against his leg.

Homer shuffled closer to Mia while the man was still doubled over. *Just grab a corner of her jacket and Einstein's shoulder and pull them both toward the door.*

"Excuse me," Mia said, raising her hand.

"No need for schoolhouse formalities around here, young lady." The man swung his arms like a conductor leading an orchestra into a crescendo. "As J.J. once said, 'We're all students and the world is a corrupted classroom from which we learn nothing but how to bring about our own undoing.'"

Mia lowered her arm. "Mr. I'm-not-sure-what-your-name-is—who's Jeremiah Whats-it?"

"You can call me Jenkins. Brother Jenkins." The man leaned against an empty display that, according to the handwritten sign above it, once held "Organic Farm-Fresh Local, Free-Range, Gluten-Free Cabbage." "I suppose I should start at the beginning. You'll have to forgive me. It's been a while since we've had prospective community members come for a tour. I'm a little rusty. Phew." Jenkins whistled. "Okay, back to the start. Brother Jeremiah was a nineteenth-century visionary. He had the foresight to see that technology would one day destroy society, and in order—"

"He thought technology in the eighteen hundreds was

bad?" Einstein interrupted. His squirming in the Banana was nothing compared to the dance he was doing now.

A cloud of confusion passed over Jenkins's face. He was clearly not used to having his pitch interrupted, but after a moment his salesman smile returned. "Brother Jeremiah had the genius to understand that the air conditioners, the airplane, plastic, were all going to—"

"But—" Einstein interrupted again. This time, he stopped shifting from one foot to the other but kept his hands pressed against the front of his pants. "Willis Carrier didn't invent the air conditioner until 1902. The Wright brothers didn't get a plane legitimately off the ground until 1903, and synthetic plastic wasn't created until Leo Baekeland made Bakelite in 1907."

Now Jenkins looked outright stunned and, Homer thought, a little panicky. "Well," he eventually spurted, "think of those examples as metaphors. So as I was saying, Brother Jeremiah saw the destructive path the world was taking and took it upon himself to lead a chosen few to salvation. He established the first of many Johacksenburgian communities in the Adirondacks in 1842. His followers achieved harmony with nature. Avoided the temptations of the world. And they all lived happily ever after."

"The end." A guy in an outfit just like Jenkins's minus the hat sauntered into the shack. "Did you tell them the next part of your inspirational spiel? About how we both gave up lucrative careers and rent-controlled apartments in Wallisburg to live off the land and be one with nature?" Each time the second guy made air quotes with his fingers, Jenkins flinched.

"Did Brother Jenkins happen to mention that there're only two members of our utopian community?" The ranting guy threw his arms in the air and turned toward Homer, Mia, and Einstein. "Did I interrupt him telling you three all about how neither one of us can farm for shit and our own parents won't join New Eden?"

"Brother Bob," Jenkins said, his teeth clenched in a pained smile. "Language. The Powers That Be would not approve."

Bob grunted and rubbed his chest. "I would give an arm for a pair of blue jeans. Hell"—he started scratching the back of his neck—"I'd give my nuts for clothing that didn't itch like I was wearing a damn sheep."

For a long, awkward moment, the only noise was the furious scraping of Bob's fingernails against his skin.

Einstein was the first one to speak. "Do you guys have a bathroom?"

"We have an outhouse," Jenkins replied brightly. "Built it ourselves from reclaimed wood."

Einstein mulled this over. "Well, I guess that's better than peeing on a tree."

"That's the spirit," Brother Jenkins said, swinging his right arm across his chest. "Just be careful on the last step and don't bother with the light switch. Someone"—Jenkins jerked his head toward Bob—"can't figure out how to properly hook up the solar panels we spent the last of my, sorry, *our* savings on."

"What are you saying about those damn panels?" Bob, still itching various parts of his body, looked up. "I told you, they're defective. It's not my fault I got sent a shoddy product."

"I wasn't even talking about them, Robert. Stop being so paranoid." Jenkins rolled his eyes. "Such a Sensitive Sally, that one."

"Okay, I'm going to go. Be right back." Einstein darted out the door Jenkins had appeared through before Homer could catch his little brother's eye and silently communicate to be quick.

"We can wait for him," Jenkins said, leaning against one of the many empty barrels that were scattered throughout the room. "The tour is short."

"Yeah, because we only have three buildings, and this dump and the stupid outhouse are two of them." Bob glowered as he backed up to the wooden pole near an empty apple bin and started rubbing against it like a bear against a tree.

Homer got the sense that Jenkins would have been throwing vegetables by now if there had been any. Jenkins's patient, happy expression was as natural as a winter storm in a snow globe. "So, what brought you in today? I bet you saw the nifty sandwich board I set by the highway."

Mia opened her mouth, paused, then shut it. *If even Mia's lost for words*—Homer didn't have the chance to finish the thought before Jenkins spoke again.

"Painted that sign myself. I imagine that you three are just the beginning of all the curious travelers who decide to pop in.”

“They didn’t see the stupid sign. No sane human beings are going to drive ten miles out of their way because of a sandwich board.” Bob stepped away from the pole, his fingers twitching as though now they too were itchy.

“People love that sign. It’s iconic,” Jenkins said, pulling a square of cloth from the chest pocket of his overalls and wiping it across his forehead.

Homer started stepping backward in the direction of the door. “Mia, maybe we should go—”

“You put it outside last Monday. How could it be iconic? Do you even know what ‘iconic’ means? Or did they not use big words at your couldn’t-get-into-the-Ivy-League-so-I-have-to-go-here safety school?” Bob’s face was as red as the cartoonish apple on the wall just over his left shoulder.

“Mia,” Homer tried again. “Let’s give—”

“Oh, come on. You’re still angry that I got in and you didn’t. Real mature, Robert. Way to get over the past.”

“Well, the eggplant on your stupid sign looks like a penis,” said Bob as he crossed his arms.

“No it doesn’t.”

“Uh, yes it does.”

“Excuse me.” Mia’s shout was strong enough to make Homer step back and loud enough to startle Jenkins and Bob into silence. “The thing is, babies can hear.” She put her hands on the sides of her stomach as though she were covering Tadpole’s ears. "So I'd rather you not shout. Plus, you two are behaving like a couple of jerk-faces. If you keep doing that, no one's going to want to join your thingie."

"Sorry." Bob scuffed his toe against the floor.

"Very sorry," Jenkins added.

"I accept." Mia kept her expression stern, but Homer could see the corners of her mouth twitch.

Except for the occasional cough and Bob's sneaker catching on the floor, the next few minutes were quiet.

When Einstein finally returned, the three of them couldn't get back to the Banana quickly enough.

Mia drove for three hours before she got tired and Homer took over. She crawled into the backseat to take a nap and Einstein moved up front.

After fifteen minutes of searching for a radio station that wasn't more static than music, Einstein turned the radio off completely, leaned his head against the window, and closed his eyes. Homer assumed he'd fallen asleep, too.

"What are you going to tell the dads when you call them later? About visiting Pillar College?"

"Oh man. I totally forgot we were supposed to do that." Homer, remembering that Mia actually was sleeping, lowered his voice to a whisper. "I thought you were down for the count." He glanced at Einstein. His little brother's eyes were still closed, but he was tapping his fingers. "I don't know. Guess I'll have to hope that they don't ask. Funny"—Homer shook his head—"I was so focused on getting out of the shack that I wasn't thinking straight. Speaking of which, why'd you take so long back there? Mia and I almost got inducted into a cult."

"Promise you won't make fun of me?" Einstein said.

"This better not be disgusting, because—"

"I was fixing their solar panels. They'd been set up wrong and it took a while to untangle all the stupid cords."

Homer swallowed. "Wow."

"Yeah." Einstein took off his glasses and polished them against his shirt. "I mean, it wasn't hard. It was a basic circuit. I learned that stuff when I was eight."

Homer formulated his response carefully. "Steiner, that was pretty awesome of you."

"Yeah?"

Homer couldn't see his little brother's expression in the dusky light, but he could hear the smile in his voice. "Yeah. Pretty much the opposite of a social fail."

Einstein slid down until he was low enough in the passenger seat to push his knees against the dashboard. "Do you think Jenkins and Bob will succeed?"

Homer stared at the yellow lines, noticing how they almost looked golden when the sun was low, thinking of an answer.

"Probably not," he said as he flipped on his left blinker for the turn onto the highway. "But they'll be able to say they tried. Maybe that'll be enough."

THE PARABLE OF
THE BOY GENIUS

THE BOY GENIUS UNDERSTOOD STRING theory, quantum mechanics, relativity, and why six of the seven Millennium Prize Problems in mathematics had yet to be solved. He did not, however, always understand other human beings.

Why did they talk so much, but rarely discuss Things That Matter: rogue artificial intelligence, meteor trajectories, the survival of humanity in an unpredictable future?

Why did old ladies bristle if he called them "old"?

Why did adults not appreciate being corrected even when they were stupendously wrong?

Why did kids his age roll their eyes when he talked and get annoyed that he walked away when they bored him?

The Boy Genius could no more help the way he was than a massive star could stop itself from exploding into a supernova.

What a gift, said strangers.

We expect great things, said his professors.

How proud you must be, said family friends to the Boy Genius's dads.

And though his dads and brother tried their best to make the world let him be a kid first and a prodigy second, they couldn't protect him from things they weren't able to see.

At the university, he tried to make friends by building scientifically sound beer funnels for parties he couldn't go to and giving sorority girls in glasses and skinny jeans answers to problem sets he could finish in ten minutes. But it wasn't exactly a social win to be the youngest guy in the classroom—never mind the smartest.

The Boy Genius often thought that it would be so much easier if people made mathematical sense. If the two sides of the equal sign did in fact equal each other.

Sometimes, when he was walking alone across campus from one science building to the next, he liked to imagine that he was an undercover anthropologist from a distant universe—a member of an advanced species who had been sent to this blue-and-green planet to observe humanity.

Being an alien offered a reason for his isolation. It allowed him to objectively observe the strange gestures and poses of *Homo sapiens*, the odd social rituals and interactions.

Sometimes, the distraction worked.

A lot of the time, it didn't.

Even extraterrestrials, it turns out, get lonely. Even Boy

Geniuses who can easily understand the complex relationships among subatomic particles, stars, space, and the dimensions of time are lost when it comes to making sense of connections here on Earth.

THE REST STOP OF
PURGATORY

"**WHY DO I FEEL LIKE** we've stumbled onto a low-budget sci-fi set? This place is creepy."

Homer nodded in agreement even though he was standing on the opposite side of the Banana and there was no way Einstein could see him. "It's the only rest stop we've seen since Maryland, so it's get money out here or leave you as collateral at the next tollbooth. That said, I think there's a strong possibility that the Otis Amos Chester Memorial Rest Stop and Museum doesn't have an ATM, which would make option two our only option."

"Very funny." Einstein paused before adding, "And, for the record, I was against stopping at a place where the bathrooms might be part of a historical exhibit."

"Duly noted," Homer replied before knocking the driver's-side door shut with his foot. He'd parked in front of a picnic area that looked both unused and worn. Three out of the four picnic tables were missing legs, and one was so deeply sunken into the dirt that its benches rested directly on the ground. The scattered evergreens and bushes hid the ugliness of the highway but were poor barriers against the gritty sounds of traffic.

"What does the sign say?" Mia bumped her shoulder against the inside of the passenger-side door, once, twice, before Homer jogged around and yanked on the outside handle. "Thanks." Mia scooted out, grabbing Homer's forearm to stand. "Phew. Watch out. Tadpole on board." She squeezed Homer's arm right above his elbow for a heartbeat and a half before walking up to a sign at the edge of the picnic area. "I can't see the letters under all the bird poo. Can you guys?" She turned around without waiting for an answer and started walking in the direction of a squatty building surrounded by drooping pine trees. "I hope they have a vending machine. I would sell my shoes for some gummies."

Einstein slid next to Homer. One side of his hair was smashed flat from napping against the window. "I'd like to point out that this place is pretty much what the world would look like after a robot apocalypse. Also, there are only three cars here and the Banana is one of them."

"Yup." Homer moved toward the small, brown building. After a beat, he heard Einstein scurry to catch up to him.

"Homer, you didn't lock the car."

"You really think I need to at this place?"

"Touché."

The parking lot was optimistically big. It was dotted with potholes, broken branches, soda cans, wrappers, and other typical roadside debris. If there had ever been white lines to indicate parking spaces, they had faded to invisible. The sign hanging off the side of the building drooped significantly lower on one side. "We're Open! Welcome to the Otis Amos Chester Memorial Rest Stop and Museum. Come on in. Please!" The "Please!" was written in red paint and glistened in places, as though it was still wet.

Homer held the door open long enough for Einstein to duck under his arm; then he followed his little brother inside.

It took a few moments for Homer's eyes to adjust to the dark once the door drifted shut behind him. When they did, he saw that the inside of the Otis Amos Chester Memorial Rest Stop and Museum was as broken-down as the outside.

The air in the small, square space felt compressed, like it was more densely packed than normal, breathable air. A water fountain between the uneven bathroom doors gurgled and sputtered. Mia and Einstein had immediately made their way to the vending machines against the far wall, and the machines' weak light made their two figures look more like fuzzy shadows than silhouettes. Displays cases lined the wall to the right, but the scratched glass covers made their contents difficult to see.

Homer's sneakers squeaked against the linoleum floor as he walked toward the closest exhibit, squinting until he could see what was inside. When he did, he was instantly sorry he'd looked. "Holy—"

"Raccoon? Ha-ha. I wish. That's only a regular ole critter. Nothin' holy 'bout him." The guy who appeared on Homer's right was dressed in brown leather pants and a matching shirt that was less a shirt and more like what people really mean when they say "tunic." He had a fur hat pulled over shiny black hair, and an obviously fake beard stuck to his tan face. "Let me introduce myself. I'm Otis Amos Chester, America's first taxidermist, depending on whom you ask." He stuck out his right hand. His fingers were long and thin; his wrist was knobby.

"Uh, hi." Homer shook the stranger's hand. "I'm Homer." Homer squinted. His eyes were still adjusting to the fluorescent lights. "Uh, do you guys have an ATM?"

"Ha-ha-ha! You people from the future with all your crazy technology!" Otis was practically shouting as he continued pumping Homer's hand up and down. "I'm afraid I have no idea what you're talking about. I'm from the eighteenth century and was one of the first people to settle the great state of Delaware, where I was definitely the first taxidermist. Some folks dispute the 'first in America' honor, but I was definitely a pioneer in the Blue Hen State." He glanced over his shoulder at a wooden door in the far-right corner. It was open just enough for a sliver of light to escape. When Otis turned back to Homer, his fake beard was askew and the fur hat low enough on his forehead to touch his eyebrows. "Ha! Ha! Ha! Yes, I learned my craft in the Old Country, coming to this great land when I was just a young whippersnapper!"

"It's been nice to meet you, Otis."

"Pleasure's all mine."

"Okay. Well, we've got to get back on the road." Homer pointed over the crazy guy's shoulder. Einstein was kicking at a vending machine's dispenser, while Mia pounded a fist against the glass. "Sorry, but can I have my hand back?"

Otis glanced at the wooden door again and then pulled Homer so close his fake beard tickled Homer's ear. "Help me," he whispered through clenched teeth and a painted-on smile.

"What?"

Otis dropped Homer's hand. "Get. Me. Out. Of. Here. I have money. I don't care where you're—and then when I was twenty-one I stuffed my first bear." His change was instantaneous. "At the old age of twenty-three, I married Miss Primrose Verity and had the privilege of preparing this fox for Benjamin Franklin's second cousin." As Otis gestured at the displays, a man dressed in a similar leather ensemble strode into the room. He was definitely much older, but he wasn't wearing a beard and his hat was nicer. Seniority, apparently, mattered at the Otis Amos Chester Memorial Rest Stop and Museum.

"Regaling our visitor with tales of your brave early years, Young Otis Amos Chester?" The man slapped Young Otis between the shoulder blades just hard enough to make him wobble for balance.

"Sure am, Old—I mean *Older*—Otis Amos Chester." Young Otis's enthusiasm was about as real as cheese that comes in a can. "In fact, I was just about to show him the gopher that might possibly have been stuffed for Mr. George Washington."

"Excellent. When you're done, I'll take our visitors to the—"

"No gummies. But they have these things called GoGo Beans." Mia shook a box of candy over her head as she slid next to Homer. "Oh, hello." If she noticed anything unusual about the two strangers' outfits, she didn't show it.

"Welcome to the Otis Amos Chester Memorial Rest Stop and Museum," Older Otis said.

"Fank too," Mia replied through a mouthful of GoGo Beans. "I lick err hasz."

Both Young Otis and Old Otis both looked puzzled. After a pause, Old Otis smiled and nodded; then Young Otis tried to do the same, but his smile looked more like a grimace.

Old Otis bowed his head slightly and was about to say something when Einstein appeared between Mia and Homer. "Thanks for the super interesting *code*. Sorry, I mean information." Einstein yanked the door open, grabbed Mia and Homer by the hands, and started tugging them outside. "We've got to get on the code—I mean the road—now."

"Are your eyes okay?" Homer asked, trying to move so

Einstein didn't knock himself over. "Why are you winking like that?"

Einstein didn't answer. Instead he called over his shoulder, "Lots of coding to do in that yellow car parked by the picnic tables."

Just before the door shut, Homer glanced back into the building. Young Otis was still smiling, and it might have been the poor lighting, but this time it looked like he meant it.

While they'd been inside the brown building, sap, needles, and a smelly greenish goop that they definitely didn't have in Florida had rained down from the tree branches onto the Banana. Mia had just slid into the driver's seat and turned on the windshield wipers when a body landed on the hood. "Ow."

Homer stepped around the side of the car, some of the paper napkins he and Einstein were using to clean off the back window held up in each hand. Young Otis peered over the Banana's hood. He had a backpack over one shoulder and had changed into jeans and a sweatshirt. "That sounded like it hurt," Homer said.

"I've done worse." Young Otis glanced over his shoulder. "Listen, we better go. I only get five-minute breaks, and once Mr. Hearst realizes I'm not experiencing digestive distress he'll be looking for me."

"Wait. What?" Homer started to drop his arms but then remembered what he was holding.

"I'm coming with you. He got the code." Young Otis pointed around Homer to Einstein, who had accumulated a small mountain of used napkins at his feet.

When Homer caught his brother's eye, Einstein shrugged. "His note came out of the vending machine with my chips. I couldn't leave a guy who writes binary-code codes." Einstein waved a slip of paper like it was a miniature flag.

"Solidarity." Young Otis pumped a fist in the air, holding it there as though he expected raised fists in return. Without the beard and hat, he looked younger than he had inside. *Closer to Einstein's age*, Homer thought.

"Wow," said Einstein. "You're even more socially awkward than I am."

Young Otis considered this for a moment before dropping his arm and shrugging in a what-can-you-do? gesture. "I've been homeschooled since I was eight and working here since I turned fourteen. To quote the great Apollo Aces, 'The universe is stacked against me. I've been down to up from the—'"

"'Start. Time will tell if it's all been worth it. Livin's its own kind of art.'" Einstein's voice cracked on "been worth it," but he was too in awe to try covering it with a cough like he usually did. "That's the third-best song on the album."

Young Otis bounced with excitement as he spoke. "Every time I go with my mom to the mall, I sneak into the music store and listen to 'Last Song of Our Lives' like a billion times. I can pretty much recite the whole album."

"That is awesome." Einstein shook his head as he scooped up the napkins at his feet and dumped them in a trash can next to the sunken picnic table. "Gross! Why do you have to listen at the mall?" Someone had written "O tush Sucks" in green spray paint around the bottom of the can.

Young Otis tapped a crushed soda can with the toe of his sneaker. "My parents are kind of strict." He looked up from the asphalt. "Which is why I really, really, *really* need to go with you guys. I don't even care where."

The driver's-side door swung open and Mia's face appeared over the Banana's roof. "Won't your parents be worried?"

"They're at a conference in Nevada. And my grandma says I need to get out more. You can even ask her. Wait. One second." Young Otis dropped his backpack on the ground, stuck his arm in practically up to his shoulder, and started digging. He didn't seem to notice or care that a pair of jeans, two comic books, and a bunch of other knickknacks spilled onto the pavement as he hunted. "Aha! Got it," he said, holding a large cell phone above his head like it was an Olympic medal. "One sec."

Young Otis jabbed his finger against the screen, then held the phone to his ear, smiling hugely the entire time. "It takes her a while to press the answer button," he whispered, covering the bottom half of the phone with his free hand. "Naniji?" he said, pulling his hand away and holding a finger up. "No, no. I have a question."

While Young Otis paced and talked, Homer dumped his

napkins in the "O tush Sucks" trash can. He stood by Einstein and watched Young Otis pace, turn, kick at trash, and then nod vigorously before sprinting around the Banana and shoving the phone at Mia.

"My grandma wants to talk to you because she thinks pregnant ladies are more responsible and less likely to be serial killers."

"Oh, that makes sense," Mia said brightly before taking the phone. "Hello?"

Young Otis shambled next to Einstein and Homer, all three of them listening to the few words Mia got in.

"Sure. Okay. Uh-huh. Yes. Very safe. I'm not sure. Let me ask." Mia put the phone against her chest. "Homer, Otis's grandma wants to know if you've ever gotten a traffic violation."

"Not even a parking ticket," Einstein shouted before Homer could open his mouth.

Mia nodded and held the phone back to her ear. "No, ma'am. Not even a parking ticket. Okay. Okay. Twice a day? I'll let him know. Okeydokey. Bye-bye." Mia hung up and turned toward where the three guys were standing in line in front of the sunken table. "Done and done." She knocked her knuckles against the Banana's roof three times. "You just need to be back before your parents are and call Grandma twice a day."

"That easy?" Homer said, looking first at Mia, then at a beaming Young Otis. "Just like that? Your grandmother?"

Young Otis shrugged. "Like I said, she's extremely worried

about my—and this is how she puts it—'real life skills.' Plus, this way she gets to watch all the American shows she doesn't get in India without any interruptions."

"Why do you want to go so badly?" Mia asked kindly as she stepped around the open door and handed Young Otis his phone.

"Thanks." Young Otis slid the phone into a front pocket. "You guys are like the first people under fifty to ever stop here, and I've never been outside of Delaware." He straightened his shoulders. "I'll be super quiet. I'm only fourteen, so I don't have my license, but I know a few things about cars."

"How do you know about cars?" Einstein was digging around on the floor of the backseat. "Aha!" He held a travel-size bottle of hand sanitizer over his head. "Today, the Earth. Tomorrow, the Galaxy." Whatever voice Einstein was trying to mimic, Homer thought he sounded more like Darth Vader before puberty than a video game hero.

"You like Apollo Aces and you play *Future Space 3000*?" Young Otis's expression was a mixture of awe and disbelief.

"Before we stopped here, I was practically going to beat level eight," Einstein replied, crossing his arms and dipping a shoulder. "I'd just gotten to the part—"

"Wait, back to the question. How do *you* know anything about cars?" Homer wanted to stop the gaming geek-out before it gained momentum. "No offense, but you seem kind of . . ." He struggled to find the nicest way to put it. "Sheltered."

Young Otis kicked a loose chunk of asphalt. It skittered a few feet before getting stuck in a pothole. "If I finish lessons early, I get out of 'school'"—he made air quotes while he said "school"—"early. The only places with people around in my neighborhood during the week are the bank, the nail place, and Arnie's Automotive. Arnie lets me hang out if I don't lean on the tire piles."

"You can come." Einstein pointed to the passenger side of the backseat. "You're over there. I'm always behind Mia. Her legs are shorter."

"Awesome." Young Otis yanked the back door open and threw himself on the seat.

He slammed the door shut as Mia slid back into the driver's seat. "Are you okay? That landing sounded like it hurt."

Homer waited until Mia shut her own door to speak. "Really, Steiner?"

"What?" said Einstein. "I feel bad for the guy. Besides, if the world ends December twentieth, don't you want to go knowing that you did something nice for a stranger?"

Einstein stuck his hands on his hips in such a way that he could have been a smaller version of D.B. A wave of homesickness hit Homer so suddenly and powerfully that he felt his eyes sting. "The world's not . . . whatever. He's your responsibility." Homer pretended to scratch his forehead so he could wipe his face before getting in the car. He had to yank on the passenger-side door three times to get it open.

Einstein whistled as he tugged at his own door. "Otis, what's your real name?"

"Siddhartha Samir Sahota, but you can call me Sid."

"So, Sid." Mia pumped the gas pedal until the Banana's engine caught. "Tell us about yourself."

Sid started talking as Mia pulled out of the Otis Amos Chester Memorial Rest Stop and Museum parking lot and didn't stop until she took a sharp left turn into the Time in a Bottle Inn in New Valor, New Jersey.

For a guy who had never been anywhere, Sid had an awful lot to say.

THE PARABLE OF THE
NEVER BEEN ANYWHERE GUY
AND THE FOUR MIRACLES

YOU CAN'T BLAME HIS PARENTS for being overprotective. After all, it was due to a series of miracles that the Never Been Anywhere Guy existed at all.

His parents met when they were not quite old, but definitely no longer young. Dr. Amanpreet Sahota was a tenured professor of religion with a large, dusty office where stacks of books sprouted like weeds, pens and student papers disappeared for years, and his computer wheezed like an asthmatic old man. Dr. Bhavjeet Batra was an art historian who specialized in the restoration of medieval tapestries, an esoteric occupation that demanded solitary days in museum basements, international travel, and fluency in three languages.

As brilliant as they were, neither one had realized the depth of his or her individual loneliness until they didn't have to be alone anymore. That both doctors were attendees at separate conferences in the same hotel in Boringville, Wyoming, and that both made the uncharacteristically impulsive decision to take a late-night swim in the indoor pool was Miracle Number One.

Miracle Number Two was that the Never Been Anywhere Guy was concocted with a mixture of science, hope, and a great deal of luck. Dr. Sahota and Dr. Batra tried the old-fashioned way to have a child. (For the record, the Never Been Anywhere Guy thought this was disgusting, and he would much prefer that his parents skip this part in the retelling of Miracle Number Two.) Then they tried shots. That was painful. Then they decided to adopt. That was frustration, forms, and red tape. Then, just as they were ready to give up completely, Dr. Batra said to Dr. Sahota, "A baby in a lab? It's a long shot. But we might as well try." Their test-tube baby was born with hair so black it looked purple under the hospital's bright lights.

Miracle Number Three happened when the Never Been Anywhere Guy was eight and he fell out of a tree. Until that day, he'd had a regular-ish childhood. Sure, his parents were higher strung than most and he couldn't eat sugar, gluten, or anything not organic. But he went to school, read comics, played soccer, and was generally kind of normal. However, when he woke up in the hospital—the fall had knocked him out—everything had changed. Seeing their son lying on the grass, unconscious, had snapped something in both Dr. Sahota and Dr. Batra.

The Never Been Anywhere Guy was homeschooled from that point on. He wasn't allowed to play sports, date, or travel on germ-ridden public transportation. Even though all his grand-parents were in their seventies, they were the ones to make the twenty-hour flight to Delaware from New Delhi instead of him going to them. And after the first time his cousins came to visit, Auntie Ujala called to complain that the little ones were walking around with thermometers in their mouths and telling other children on their street that that was what all American kids did.

The Never Been Anywhere Guy grew up to be a restless fourteen-year-old who was desperate to go *somewhere, everywhere, anywhere.* Maybe it was the scratchy beard and leather pants he had to wear for the job his parents had lined up for him, a job he hated. Or maybe it was something larger. Maybe seeing three kids who looked around his age spill out of an ugly yellow sedan was the tipping point, the final push he needed to tighten the mishmash of seclusion, curiosity, and boredom inside him into an unbearable ball studded with broken bits. Suddenly, he knew that he had to go and this might be his only chance.

That the three strangers agreed to take him became Miracle Number Four.

THE INN WHERE TIME STOPPED AND BEGAN

"**SHOOT.**" **HOMER TRIPPED OVER** a wrinkle in the mud-colored carpet for the second time since he, Einstein, and Sid had entered room 117 at the Time in a Bottle Inn. With this stumble, instead of falling face-first onto one of the double beds, he sent his cell phone flying across the room and had to reach behind a scratched nightstand to retrieve it.

"D.B., you there? Yeah. Sorry. This room is trying to kill me." To be safe, Homer decided to move his pacing to the worn patch of linoleum in front of the bathroom.

"Yeah," he said. "It's actually not the worst place we've stayed in." Homer was too tired to recount Einstein's detailed description of the swampy smell of the bedspreads and the look on Sid's face when he slid off the bed closest to the door and found a dirty sock and a sticky mug underneath.

"Uh-huh. No, like I said, Sid's really nice. Yeah, he's amazed by everything. I doubt that he's ever slept in a scuzzy hotel. He got way too excited about the free soap. He thinks Einstein is the coolest guy in the world, so that's something." Homer caught a glimpse of himself in the bathroom mirror. Just enough to make him pause and stare back at the guy with a phone pressed to his ear. His hair was the longest it'd been since he was a little kid. When he ran his hand over his head, he looked like a blond porcupine.

"What do you mean? Like, what we've seen on purpose or just in general?" Homer hated this question. It was so simple, but when D.B. asked it each night, he struggled to answer. How could he possibly condense all the small, epic, weird, funny, and bizarre things that he'd seen into a few sentences? Out loud, he gave D.B. a vague rundown, while somewhere else in his brain he tried to take stock. That day alone, they'd stopped at six different gas stations, eaten at four different fast-food places, spotted two abandoned sofas by the side of the highway, and driven by more roadkill than anyone should have to see in a lifetime.

They'd passed a scarecrow in a tuxedo, a rusted swing set lying on its side under an overpass, and a child's dress shoe with frayed black laces that swung side to side like a waving hand. He could tell D.B. about all these things, but explaining how each one of them was so much bigger than what he was saying felt impossible, so he changed the topic instead.

"Have you heard anything from Chief Harvey about the lot?"

The knock at the door couldn't have come at a better time as far as Homer was concerned. "Wait a second, I think Einstein and Sid lost their key card. Uh-huh. No, just the vending machines. Sid eats nonstop." He pulled the door open harder than he meant to. "Oh, hey."

Mia had changed into pajamas that were long enough to cover her bare feet right to the toes and a green sweatshirt that fell a few inches above her knees. Her hair was piled on top of her head in a way that cast half her face in shadow. She looked so obliviously beautiful, Homer felt like he'd been punched.

Mia's surprised expression turned into an apology when she saw that Homer had his phone pressed to his ear. "I'm so sorry. I'll come back. In the morning."

"Wait," Homer called, but Mia had already started walking away. "No, sorry, D.B. I was talking to Mia. What? Good. Yeah. Happy. Listen, I'm going to go. Steiner has his phone on him. No, if you call enough times he'll pick up. Yup. Yup. Love you, too."

Homer slid his phone into his pocket, and then a key card. He tried to get his hair to lie flat but gave up after just a few swipes. He pulled the door shut behind him with a click, padded down the springy and surprisingly clean hall carpet to Mia's room five doors down, and knocked

Mia opened her door slowly. "Hey. I'm sorry. You didn't need to stop talking."

Suddenly, Homer didn't know where to look. Meeting

Mia's eyes seemed too intense, but staring over her would be rude. He settled for looking down at his shoes and her feet. The pink polish on Mia's toenails was chipped and the ink tattoo she'd doodled on the bridge of her right foot that morning had already faded. An awkward amount of time passed before Homer could get his brain to stop racing and his mouth to respond. "No worries. D.B. would have kept me on the phone for hours, so I should be thanking you for saving me."

Mia smiled and tried to wipe flyaway strands of hair off her face. "Long hair is so annoying." She caught a few strands and tucked them behind one ear just as others drifted free. "Do you want to come in?" She opened the door wider.

"Yeah, sure." As Homer walked by Mia, he stretched out his hand, and, without realizing what he was doing, he brushed the newly loose strands behind her right ear. "It's hard to get it all without a mirror. Not that I know, but I imagine it's hard." He dropped his hand. Cleared his throat and silently prayed that the light in Mia's room was as terrible as the light in his.

"My hair is easy. It's stuff like reaching behind me or painting my toes that's near impossible. Now that I've got to work around the watermelon in front of me." Mia shut the door and hopped onto the bed, folding her legs to the side.

Homer sat down in an office chair by the window, catching his feet against the desk to keep from spinning. "When you jump around like that, it's easy to forget you're pregnant."

"True story: I sometimes forget, too." Mia shifted backward

until she was leaning against the headboard. "Not a lot, but sometimes. It's funny." She yanked the elastic out of her hair, put it between her teeth, and gathered the waves of red back on the top of her head as she spoke. "I fwought I'd be terrify but I rembwer and"—she grabbed the elastic with one hand and twisted her hair until she once again had a messy bun—"it makes me happy."

"Do girls know how amazing it is when they do that?" Homer asked. "It's like you're all secret hair ninjas. Swoop, swoop, twist, and done."

"Ha." Mia giggled and chucked a striped throw pillow at Homer, who caught it and stuck it behind him.

"Thanks. I needed lower back support." He put his feet up on the desk, his hands behind his head, and leaned back like he was in a beach chair.

"Homer, do you think I'll be a good mom?" Mia looked down at her hands, twirling the large silver ring she wore on her right pointer finger.

Homer dropped his feet to the floor. "That came out of nowhere. Of course I do. You're going to be a great mom."

"Why?" Mia looked up, and even in the crappy light from the crappy lamps, Homer could see that she was biting the sides of her mouth, trying not to cry. "How do you know?"

"Because you're kind and thoughtful and really, really patient." Homer tapped his knuckles against the office chair's armrests. "You're pretty much the only person in the world who Einstein hasn't lost his marbles with. And that's because you listen to him each time as though you haven't heard his theories a million times before and as though everything he's saying isn't outrageous."

Mia sniffed and then wiped her eyes against her sleeve. "He's so smart and I want Tadpole to be smart." Mia dropped her arm and looked down at her hands again. Her voice was scratchy, each word a burr that caught in her throat. "I don't want him—or her—to be dumb like me. I want better." Mia's eyes searched Homer's face like she was worried about what she'd find. "I'm not asking for Tadpole to be a genius, but I want her, him, to be happy and safe and . . . I don't want to mess up. I don't want to be like my mom. And I'm so scared that—" Mia closed her eyes and breathed in and out twice before she opened them. "I need you to know that I don't feel sorry for myself. Other people have had it way worse than me. I don't want you to think that—"

"Mia." Homer's brain and heart were both reeling, but for once the right words came to him. "I think that's what most parents—the good ones—all want: to give their kids the best life possible."

"Yeah." Mia sniffed as she rubbed at her eyes with a fist.

"Yeah," Homer said, pulling a handful of tissues from the box on the desk. He sat on the side of the bed near the window and held them out.

"Thank you." Mia grabbed a tissue and wiped it across her face. "I'm a mess. Ugh, this is super, super embarrassing."

"Nah. I'm actually surprised you haven't cried more." Homer shifted so he was facing Mia. "When Christian's friend Lisa was pregnant, she cried all the time. I used to keep travel packs of tissues in my pockets whenever she visited." He looked down at his hands, pressing his right thumb on top of his left, then switching. *One way. Then the other. Repeat until calm.* "The fact that you're worried about being a good mom is its own proof that you'll be great."

Mia grabbed another tissue and began pulling its layers apart. "Why are you so nice to me, Homer?" The tissue fragments drifted like white flower petals onto the floor beside the bed.

"Because you deserve to have people be nice to you." Homer responded without thinking—like the answer had been formed months ago and waiting to be used ever since.

Mia sniffed. "You deserve good things, too." She picked up another tissue and tore it into smaller and smaller pieces. Once she had a pile, she gathered the tissue petals in her left hand and let them trickle between her fingers across the carpet. "Homer, will you stay? Just until I fall asleep. Tadpole kicks . . . and sometimes it's hard to sleep."

Homer was afraid the trembling in his chest would rattle his words. All he dared to say was "Okay."

"Okay." Mia swept the last of the tissues off the comforter and slid under it.

Homer placed his sneakers side by side underneath the desk. He slid his phone out of his pocket and sent a quick series of texts to Einstein:

Don't worry.

With Mia.

She was upset.

Don't stay up too late.

Everything's fine.

He got only one reply:

Okay! But I'm taking your bed. ;)

Homer turned his phone to silent, then shut the lamps off one by one. He had to grab the bedspread twice before his fingers remembered how to work. Still in his jeans and T-shirt, he slid under the comforter as quietly as he could. "Night, Mia."

"Sweet dreams, Homer," Mia whispered into her pillow.

Homer stared at the digital clock on the nightstand, wishing he could make the numbers stop changing, until Mia's breath slowed into a gentle rise and fall.

He was willing himself to slide out of the bed, put on his shoes, and make his way back down the carpeted hallway when Mia sat up. She wiggled her sweatshirt over her head, tossed it on the floor, and then shifted under the covers until her back touched Homer's chest. Without saying a thing, she reached for his hands and wrapped his arms around her, and without saying a thing in return, Homer pulled her close enough to feel her hair drift across his face. Her shoulder blades pressed against his rib cage from the outside. His wildly happy heart pressed from within.

Not long after, they both fell asleep.

In the morning, everything was different.

LOOKING FOR HOPE
ON THE HUDSON

"WE'RE DEFINITELY GOING THE RIGHT way. I recognize this part. My parents always stopped here when we used to visit. There's the sign for the boring art gallery my mom loved. There's the church my dad made us tour." Sid had managed to wedge his face between Homer's headrest and the driver's-side window, which meant he'd been shouting directions in Homer's left ear for most of the morning.

Homer didn't care. He was only half listening to Sid anyway. Mia seemed similarly distracted. In the Time in a Bottle Inn parking lot that morning, she'd been the first one to say yes when Sid suggested they drive through New York State and stay with his mother's cousin for a night. When Einstein pointed out how far out of the way they'd be going, Mia said she didn't care. She wasn't in a rush. Then her eyes met Homer's. She had smiled. And he had smiled back.

"Homer? Come in, Homer." A plastic dinosaur hit the

dashboard, then bounced into Homer's lap. "Are you asleep?"

"No," Homer said, picking up the miniature T. rex and tossing it back at Einstein. "Where did that come from?"

"Toy vending machine," Einstein replied. "Homes, I know it's foggy out, but I think you can drive faster than this. You've managed to create traffic on a two-lane road and pretty soon folks are going to start honking."

"I have?" Homer glanced in his rearview mirror. The line of cars behind him stretched so far back that the fog made it impossible to see the end. "Wow." He shook his head. "Sorry, guys. I'm going to pull over and let these people pass." Homer steered the Banana off to the side, and before he could put it in park, cars were zipping by and quickly disappearing around the next bend.

"Homes, you okay?" Sid asked as he flopped back into his seat. "You seem out of it, and I should warn you that my mom's cousin is a naturopath, and if you so much as sneeze in her presence, she'll make you drink some kind of nasty medicine."

"Good to know, but I'm fine. Just tired." When Homer glanced in the rearview mirror, he caught Einstein smirking. "Steiner, what's so—"

"Look!" Mia interrupted. "It's beautiful."

"What? What?" Sid's bouncing caused the Banana's leather seats to protest. "That wasn't a fart. I swear."

"An angel," Mia said as she leaned over Homer. Her face was so close to his that he could feel the warmth radiating off her cheek. "A statue. Stone, I think."

Homer tried to shift without Mia's noticing. Her right elbow was digging into the soft spot above his knee, but he didn't want her to think she had to move. "I don't see it."

"There." Mia jabbed her finger against Homer's window.

He followed her pointer finger and waited for a break between the clouds of fog. When one came, he saw the stone cross with a winged figure on top nested in the trunk of a solitary tree. It was surrounded by a half circle of stuffed animals, flowers in various stages of decay, and envelopes and other pieces of paper.

"It's like the tree is swallowing the statue." With his sleeve, Homer wiped the circle his breath made on the window. "The angel's wings are already part of the trunk and roots have curled up around the base, but the stuff on the ground, some of it anyway, is brand-new."

"It's been here long enough for the tree to grow around the stone, but not so long that people have forgotten about the person it's for. They remember, and they're still sad enough to visit," Einstein whispered, his breath also making little fog circles on his window. "'Fly free, our sweet angel,'" Einstein said. "Whew. That's heavy."

The backseat squeaked and Einstein mumbled something incomprehensible.

"That's what it says on the cross?" Sid asked. "Does that mean there was an accident here?"

"My oldest brother, foster brother, Jacob, crashed a car once," Mia whispered, zigzagging her finger across Homer's window. "His friends put something up on the side of the road, but it wasn't this nice. I think they tried to plant a tree, but it died. No one took care of it enough."

Mia shoved herself off Homer's lap. "I'm going to go take a picture." She grabbed one of the disposable cameras from the passenger-side floor, shoved her door open, and then nudged it shut with her hip. She tore the plastic wrapper off the unopened camera as she marched in front of the car and across the road toward the angel in a tree, but when she stopped a foot or so from the collection of gifts and weathered letters, Mia didn't take any pictures. Instead she slid the camera into her coat pocket, stood still, and looked. When the fog and drizzle turned to rain, she moved the stuffed animals, envelopes, and paper scraps closer to the angel and the trunk of the tree. Even after that, Mia stayed a few minutes longer, watching to make sure the gifts were protected and that she had done everything she could.

Sid was the first one to speak once the lights of Hopeville-on-the-Hudson became visible halfway across the River's End Bridge. "This part I don't remember. It looks so fragile, like the whole city is one sneeze away from falling in the river. Plus, I swear there was a diner right after the bridge."

"All those lights. Like a tree, a giant Christmas tree," said Mia as she craned her neck and pressed her face against her window to see as much of the city perched on the side of the riverbank as she could. "It's so pretty. Be even prettier if I had a milkshake right now. I'm so, so hungry."

The only thing Homer could think to add was that Hopeville-on-the-Hudson was the strangest place he'd ever seen. But that observation seemed bland after Sid's and Mia's, so Homer said, "Yeah," and kept his thought to himself.

Hopeville-on-the-Hudson wasn't a tall city of skyscrapers, asphalt, and glitz like the one they'd driven by that afternoon. Rather, it was a place of stunted shoulder-to-shoulder structures, brick, and hazy streetlights that were far too weak to offend the dusk. Hopeville stretched up and away from the Hudson River's bank as if the buildings had all grown from a handful of tossed seeds: tightly packed near the water's edge and spreading farther and farther apart as the land sloped upward. Maybe once upon a time it had been a shiny, hopeful city, but that night, with the river as black as oil and the row of warehouses with windows that stared over the water like sleepy eyes, Hopeville looked more like a haunted place than anything else.

Homer took the first exit at the end of the bridge and then his first left, trying to find a place to park while Sid got oriented. If there was any order to the narrow streets, the four of them couldn't figure it out. The streets made curved lines instead of straight, ended abruptly, and went from two-way to one-way without any warning. No matter which direction Homer turned, they kept going downhill toward the water.

The Banana had made it all the way to the row of warehouses with the spooky window eyes when the sound coming from the engine went from the occasional thump to a drum solo.

"What is—" Before Mia could finish her question, the engine released one more thunderous boom and stopped just before a burp of black smoke erupted from under the hood.

"Uh, Sid," Homer said, staring at the tendrils of smoke as they blended into the darkening sky. "Do you have any idea what just happened?"

"Without looking under the hood, my best guess is firecrackers in the engine."

"Ha," Einstein snorted. "That would be insane."

"Right?" Sid replied. "Or just skip the firecrackers and get your hands on some pure magnesium—"

"No way, you'd want sulfur and potassium nitrate for the rotten eggs smell."

"Guys." Mia turned as much as her seat belt and stomach would let her. "I love fireworks, but I am five minutes away from cranky-pantsville if I don't get something to eat soon, so if we could focus on the problem at hand, that would be super."

"Wow." Einstein unclicked his seat belt and scooted toward the center of the backseat. "That was the most serious I've ever seen you."

"It was scary," Sid added.

"Sorry, Sid." Mia patted her stomach. "It's just when I get hungry, I turn into an— Holy Jesus!" Mia jumped so far back from her window that her left elbow knocked an hours-old lidless Slurpee cup out of the cup holder and into Homer's lap.

Homer didn't know whether to react to the sticky electric-green puddle he was sitting in or to the face with sunglasses that had just appeared outside Mia's open window.

"Nah, but I've been mistaken for him a time or two. It's the sandals." The wiry guy in sunglasses flung one of his feet high enough to be even with the side mirror. "And the hair." He set his foot back on the ground and peered in the window. He had a long nose, and his shoulder-length hair was somewhere between yellow and orange. "Looks like you all are in a pickle." His voice sounded worn, like his words bumped and bruised one another as they traveled from his brain to his mouth.

"Sorry," Mia gasped. "You surprised me." She looked over her shoulder at Homer. "Oh no. Did I do that?" She pointed at the wet circle spreading across Homer's pants.

The Jesus Guy spoke before Homer could. "I should be the one apologizing, Little Mama." He stood up and made a gesture like he was tipping a hat. "Shouldn't have snuck up on you like that." He braced his hands against his knees so his face was once again in the center of Mia's window. "You kids visiting?"

"Where? Here?" Einstein's head appeared between the front seats.

"Guess that answers my question." The Jesus Guy pushed himself to standing. Despite the cold, he was dressed in cargo shorts and a brightly striped poncho. "I just assumed you were heading to Renata's. That's where most folks are going when they get down here. You should stop in. Queen Bee likes a full house."

Homer shifted his way forward to the edge of his seat. The Slurpee had soaked almost completely into his pants, and each movement he made sounded like a boot lifting out of mud. "That's really nice of you, but we're expected somewhere. If you could give us directions, though, we'd appreciate it."

"Uh, Homer?" Sid interrupted.

"Yeah?"

"I think I mixed things up."

The Slurpee's sweet smell and the rubber stench of smoke suddenly seemed overwhelming. For a second Homer thought he was going to throw up. "Okay?"

"I just got a text from my grandmother," Sid said, his voice tentative, uneven. "I guess my mom's cousin's in Hudsonville-on-the-Hudson, not Hopeville, which is definitely a way better name."

Homer rested his head on the steering wheel. He put his sticky hands together, then thought better about placing them any closer to his face. When he spoke, the words rattled. "So you're telling me the engine just blew, it's nighttime, and we're in the completely wrong place?"

"Not completely wrong. We're on the correct side of the river. Look."

In his peripheral vision, Homer saw Sid's outstretched arm

jiggling a phone. He sat up and let his head drop so he was looking at the car ceiling. "Sir, is there any chance there's a service
station nearby?"

"Ha, you're funny, big guy." The Jesus Guy raised his arms
straight out from his sides and tilted his head back as if he was
addressing the sky. "Welcome to the river's edge, where things
get bent but seldom straightened and crime is its own currency."
As if to punctuate his sentence, a crack, followed by the sound
of breaking glass and slamming metal, cut through the night.
The Jesus Guy dropped his arms, swiped his sunglasses off, and
leaned in Mia's window.

"Look, if you all don't mind pushing for a bit, Martha used
to be a mechanic, and she's always at Renata's on . . . what day
is it?" He pulled a phone out of one of his many pockets. The
light from the screen gave his face a blue tint and made his nose
seem even longer. "Wednesday. In fact, I'm already late in picking her up." He slid the phone back into his pocket. "Martha'll
be too tuned up to do anything tonight, but she can take a look
under the hood first thing in the morning. She's guaranteed
to be hungover, but phew"—he whistled—"even at her worst,
Martha's just that good."

Mia stuck her hand out the window. "I'm Mia."

"Pleased to meet ya, Mia. They call me Poncho." He shook
Mia's hand and then stood up. "You don't have to wait at Queen
Bee's, but you definitely want to get your car off the street."
Poncho patted the Banana's roof. "Can't see anyone wanting

this beauty whole, but even a crappy chop shop could do something with the parts. How about you put her in neutral and then we'll push her a couple of blocks?"

"All righty." Mia scooted out of the car before Homer had even undone his seat belt.

Unsticking himself from the front seat was disgusting and messy, but once Homer stood up, he wished he were still sitting behind the wheel in a pool of Slurpee.

"Wow," said Sid, bouncing out of the backseat. "It looks like you electric-green peed your pants."

"Thanks," Homer replied, trying to wipe some of the stickiness off his hands and onto his T-shirt.

"Your pee can be green?" The orange glow from the streetlight Mia was standing under made her eyes seem exceptionally large.

Homer was grateful that Poncho chose that moment to start giving orders.

"Hey, Little Dude."

Einstein opened the left back door and leaned out. "Uh-huh."

"Today you get your driver's license. You're gonna steer while we push."

If Einstein hesitated, it was only for a moment. "Okay." He rooted around on the floor of the backseat until he found a large sweatshirt and some magazines. He threw them over the driver's seat on top of the spilled Slurpee and then slid over the center console, landing in a tangle behind the steering wheel.

"Okay, put it in neutral and let's go." Poncho gestured for Homer and Sid to line up next to him behind the Banana.

"I feel pretty useless right now. I can at least steer," Mia said as she crossed her arms and kicked at the ground, sending pebbles skittering over the uneven sidewalk.

"Don't worry about it. Between Bean Pole, Big Dude, and me, we got this." Poncho braced his hands against the back bumper, waiting for Homer and Sid to do the same on either side of him. "On my count we're gonna push this thing like it insulted our mamas. Okay?"

"Okay." Homer adjusted his feet. "My name's Homer, by the way. That's Sid." Homer gestured with his chin.

"Howdy." Sid gave a little wave, then went back to his pushing stance.

"And the driver's my little brother. His name is—"

"Nobody goes by their given names at the Collective. Down here"—Poncho shifted his feet—"you all are Big Guy, Bean Pole, Little Dude, and Little Mama."

"Is 'the Collective' the garage?"

"Nope. That's what we call Renata's—Queen Bee's—place. Get ready. One. Two. Three. Push." The Banana shot forward.

"We're moving." Einstein's face in the side mirror was almost split in half with an enormous grin.

"Little Dude, steer straight until I tell you to turn." Poncho grunted. "Shit. This thing is a boat. Great paint job, though."

Neither Homer nor Sid had the breath to disagree, so the

two of them grunted and Poncho swore and hooted and Einstein steered and Mia shouted encouragements and, step by step, they pushed the world's most hideous car down a poorly lit street somewhere in a city called Hopeville-on-the-Hudson.

THE KINDNESS OF STRANGERS IN A CITY CALLED HOPE

PONCHO HAD EINSTEIN STEER THE Banana through the entrance of a large brick building with concrete pillars and walls covered in graffiti. Then he pointed to a similar building directly across the street and promised he'd see them there in a few hours.

"What just happened?" asked Sid.

No one was able to answer, so they picked up their bags and walked single file to the steps leading up to a large, dented metal door.

Mia was the first one up the stairs. She ran her finger down the list of tenants and apartment numbers. "Renata. Apartment four," she read. "I wonder if she has a last name." Mia pressed a button under the intercom, holding it down until a crackling sound came out of the speaker, followed by buzzing loud enough to make Einstein jump and hit his elbow on the stair's metal railing.

"Ow. Ow. Ow." Einstein held his left elbow in his right hand and tried to speak through gritted teeth. "I think . . . we're . . . ow . . . supposed to do something with the—" Einstein was cut off by three things: a man and a woman yelling at each other on the corner, the intercom crackling a second time, and the jackhammer-like buzzing once again pounding the air.

Before all the noise stopped, Mia pushed the door, it opened, and then she stepped inside. After a brief hesitation, Sid, Homer, and, finally, Einstein followed her.

"Sweet Mother of Jesus," a voice echoed down the metal stairs as the door swung shut behind Einstein. "I was about to come down there and scream at the kids from Albany Street for playing ding-dong ditch. What took you so long?" The woman who clicked down the stairs and stopped on the first landing had on pink platform heels, black pants, an artfully torn jacket, and a bemused smile that rose higher on one side of her heavily made-up face than the other. "Come on in." She spun and started clicking upward. Her movements languid and yet quick.

"Renata, right?" Sid practically bounced up the first steps. "This is where you live? Phew. There's a lot of stairs. Have you ever counted them? How'd you know we were coming?" Mia, Einstein, and Homer were much slower to reach the top floor. When they did, the woman was still answering Sid's questions.

". . . Yes, the whole fourth floor is mine. I have no idea how many stairs. I just know that the elevator is as reliable as my ex-boyfriend. Finally, I knew to expect you because Poncho texted me. Okay, questions answered. Now, before you enter, you should know three things." Their guide's long nails clicked against the door handle as she spoke. "One, this door isn't as heavy as it looks, so stand back when I open it. Two, the place is a mess. And three . . . hmmm." She put a hand on her hip. "Can't remember, so it must not be important." She planted her heels, flung the door open, and swung one arm in a grand gesture before stepping inside.

"Welcome, welcome." The lights flickered before catching, revealing a large open space that once must have held rows and rows of massive machines. The ceiling rose to a shallow vault and the concrete floor was marked by divots and cracks that the mismatched carpets did little to disguise. Slumped sofas, one of them with tire marks across the cushions, dominated three corners, and a circle of beanbag chairs held court near dramatically large windows that overlooked a small park and the river. To call the area nearest the door a kitchen would be generous. The refrigerator, table, plastic chairs, cupboards, and scarred stove looked like they had been dropped from a plane and just happened to land next to one another.

"This is all yours?" Mia didn't wait for Renata to answer. "It's like a playhouse. Like the kind of place you imagined living in as a little kid, you know?" She spun in a slow circle, her eyes wide like she was afraid of missing something, stopped, and drifted toward the windows. "Holy Toledo." She stood on tiptoe and pressed her forehead against the glass. "You can see for miles and miles, and there's the bridge we drove over, and a swing set."

Homer didn't know if his feet acted without his head or if the thought happened so quickly he missed it completely, but suddenly he was standing next to Mia, stopping his hand just before it tugged on her sleeve to pull her away from the window. She stepped back a beat later.

"Homer, what's wrong? You're sweating. Right here." Mia trailed her fingers down the side of Homer's face. "Are you okay?"

Homer nodded and Mia took an extra step away from the windows.

"Where's the TV?" Einstein said, stepping onto a thin purple-and-gold carpet. He glanced at his feet. "Is this supposed to be the living room? Does anyone actually use that?" He pointed to a claw-foot bathtub in the far corner.

"All of you, so curious." Renata clicked her tongue. "Let's say we start with names and then go from there." She nodded at Mia. "Ladies first."

"I'm Mia Márquez and this is Tadpole Márquez." She patted her stomach.

"Cute. Next."

"I'm Homer Finn."

"Hi. My name is Siddhartha Samir Sahota, but you can call me Sid."

"Will do, Sid. And you?" She pointed at Einstein.

"I'm Einstein Finn. Homer's my brother."

"Oh, that's too perfect. That makes me Renata, but Poncho's probably been calling me Queen Bee." She used the kitchen counter for balance as she took off her heels. "Ah. So much better. I don't normally wear them around the house, but I need to break these in for a new show." Renata looked up. "Sid, sweetheart, better close your mouth. Don't want to catch any flies in there."

Sid snapped his mouth shut faster than a screen door with spring hinges. "Sorry. I'm from Delaware. I don't get out much. Uh, you're really pretty." He turned to Einstein. "Is that an S.F.?"

"Aren't you a sweet thing." Renata clapped her hands. "It took me a while to . . . let's say 'find' this look, so your words are like honey for a bear."

"Find?" Mia asked, studying the shapes in the faux marble countertop.

Renata tilted her head. "Poncho didn't explain anything, did he?" As Renata stepped by him, Homer saw that she was younger than her thick makeup made her seem—maybe five years, ten tops, older than him. Her broad nose and square jaw drew attention to her full lips and sharp cheekbones. Her eyelashes were thick, black, and unabashedly fake. "You'll have to forgive him. He's sweetly oblivious."

"Already forgiven," Mia said, glancing up from the countertop. "Did you know you have fish in your counter?" Mia moved her pointer finger one place, then another. "Here and here."

"I did not. I think I found a small bird in the floor by the sink. All sorts of critters to be found in scratched linoleum."

Sid still looked confused. "I don't want to be rude, but can I ask—"

"I bet I already know the question, Sid from Delaware." Renata flopped on one of the low couches. "I was born a boy. Grew up in a great big city. But that city and that skin didn't fit me too well, so now I'm Renata." She snorted. "Just another talented lady who looks good in sequins. A waitress by day. Cabaret singer by night."

"Actually," Sid said, staring at his feet and blushing, "I was going to ask how you walk in those shoes." He pointed at the abandoned heels.

"Lord, that'll teach me to make assumptions." Renata's laughter echoed in the cavernous space. "The answer is practice. I've been practicing for heels most of my life."

Mia raised her hand. "I have a question."

"You are adorable. I might have an answer," Renata replied, curling her legs up on the couch.

"Why are you being so nice to us? Wait. That sounds wrong. Let me try again." Mia closed her eyes, breathed in and out, opened her eyes, and tried again. "What I meant to say is: We're strangers and you don't know us and we're in your apartment. Why?" Mia chewed at her thumbnail.

Renata leaned back, supporting her head with one hand. She studied Mia's face, then Einstein's, then Sid's, and finally Homer's, lingering a little longer on him than she had on any of the others'. Homer wasn't sure whether that was a good or a bad thing, or why she winked at him before turning back to Mia. "Darling, when it comes to people, I've learned to trust my instinct, and she's telling me you all have good hearts. As to why I'm helping strangers, I'll give you the short answer: once upon a time, a gracious lady did a nice thing for me and that nice thing changed my life. Now, I believe in paying it forward. If I can help some travelers who, miraculously, break down on my block, well then I'm just giving back a modicum of what the universe has given to me."

"What did she do, the nice lady?" Mia asked.

"She told me I could stay. And then, years and years later, she gave me a way to leave."

"Oh." Mia looked as confused as Homer felt, but neither one of them asked anything more.

"Now, since your car won't be fixed until Martha takes a look in the a.m., why don't you get yourselves settled?" She glanced at Homer. "If you want to clean up, there's a curtain that pulls around the tub, and a washing machine in the basement."

Homer had forgotten about the spilled Slurpee. Most of his front was still wet, but whatever had dried acted like glue, sticking his pants to his skin.

"We'll have to pull out the beds—just mattresses, really—but the slumber party won't start for a long while." Renata padded across the room toward a wardrobe covered in bumper stickers. "I bet you all are starving," she said, flinging open the wardrobe doors. "I am so sick of all these old things." She started pulling out dresses, shirts, skirts, tank tops, dropping each onto a pile at her feet. "I can't cook worth a damn, but I have Buddha's Delight on speed dial. You four like Chinese?" She didn't wait for an answer. "I told people to start coming by at ten, but no one will get here before eleven. You can put money on that." Renata shook her head. "One would think that being fashionably late would have gone out of style once *everybody* started doing it."

"There's a party? Here? Is it your birthday?" Mia asked.

"You are just sweet enough to eat. No, darling. We're alive and it's a Wednesday night in a city called Hope. In my opinion, those are reasons enough to throw a party."

THE PARABLE OF THE
GIRL WHO WOULD CHOOSE
HER OWN NAME

THE GIRL WHO WOULD CHOOSE Her Own Name wished she had stronger memories of growing up in Rio and being little and being okay. It'd be so lovely to fall into the recesses of her mind and go back to when the labels "boy" and "girl" meant as much to her as the differences between the various purple crayons. (It wasn't important whether you called the color "amethyst," "grape," or "aubergine." What mattered was the creation of pictures.)

Unfortunately, the human mind can hold only so much, and the memories hers clung to, the ones that were so willing to push their way to the surface again and again, came largely from After. After her mother, grandmother, and she left Rio. After the three of them settled in a small apartment in the poorest borough of the largest city in America. After she started feeling angry that she had to answer to a name (a boy's name) that wasn't hers, not really.

She could remember sadness, how her inside-self used to rattle against the walls of its outside-self like a penny in an empty can. The messed-up mantra *This is not my body. This is not my body* on constant repeat at the very front of her brain.

When the Girl Who Would Choose Her Own Name was ten, she told her *avó*, her grandmother, that God had made a mistake. She was supposed to be a girl, not a boy. Even though it was Saturday and so early that morning cartoons hadn't started, Avó gave her a swat on her butt and sent the Girl Who Would Choose Her Own Name to the tiny bedroom she shared with her mother to ask God for *perdão*.

When her *mãe* came home from cleaning rich people's apartments, the Girl Who Would Choose Her Own Name was still in the bedroom, looking out the window that faced the street and praying—but not for forgiveness.

Mãe stood in the doorway watching the Girl Who Would Choose Her Own Name, and by looking at the dresser mirror, the Girl was able to watch her mother, too. Years and years before that moment, when they had still lived in Rio with Papai, Mãe's hair had been shiny and black. Now it was streaked with gray. Life had begun to mark Mãe's pretty face, appearing as thin lines across her forehead, purple half circles beneath her eyes, bite marks on her lips. The Girl Who Would Choose Her Own Name hated that she added to the invisible weights that pressed down on Mãe's shoulders.

Later that night, once Avó had gone into the second bedroom, Mãe asked if the Girl Who Would Choose Her Own Name would like to come to work with her on Saturdays from now on. She could use the help, and Avó might be less cranky if she got to watch her *telenovelas* instead of cartoons.

Most of the time, Mãe's clients weren't home when she came to clean. They were out working, vacationing, eating at fancy restaurants, shopping for fancy things. But one lady was always home. She was sick, she explained. She didn't go out much. Not like she used to.

The Sick Lady didn't mind if the Girl Who Would Choose Her Own Name accompanied her mother. In fact, she would pay her to help her sort through the files in the library. The Sick Lady said she wanted to have her affairs in order before her time came. That was what she said. Word for word. "Before. Her. Time. Came."

The Sick Lady looked like her bones could poke through her skin, and her body was marked by strange lumps and bruises that she tried to hide with swishy pants and bracelets that clicked and clacked. At first, the Sick Lady and her library scared the Girl Who Would Choose Her Own Name. Both seemed haunted by memories and ghosts.

But after a few months of Saturdays, her afternoons with the Sick Lady became the best part of the Girl Who Would Choose Her Own Name's week.

As they went through her files and books, the Sick Lady told the Girl Who Would Choose Her Own Name all about "Before," when she had sung in clubs all over "the City." She had worn glittering dresses and had stood by glistening pianos. Her fans followed her uptown, downtown, across the river, and to all five boroughs. Strangers sent her flowers and marriage proposals. But, she said, success wasn't enough to keep the past from creeping in, armed with its favorite weapons: guilt and regret. Sad memories made her do stupid and desperate things, things that would momentarily tame the monster trapped in her chest. These things were the reason she was sick. If she could go back, she said, she would have faced her sadness—tried to understand it instead of always pushing it out of the way.

The Girl Who Would Choose Her Own Name didn't get what the Sick Lady meant one hundred percent of the time, but she loved the melody of her voice and the elegant words she used. Good things were "exquisite." Bad ones "deplorable." Nothing was so-so. The Sick Lady did not believe, she explained, in "in-betweens."

As the Girl Who Would Choose Her Own Name got older and was allowed to take the subway on her own, she sometimes went to the Sick Lady's apartment without Mãe. On those days, they didn't work. Instead they watched old movies and played old music, and the Sick Lady would talk and the Girl Who Would Choose Her Own Name would listen.

The last time the Girl Who Would Choose Her Own Name saw her friend, the Sick Lady was lying in bed with beeping machines, tubes, and orange pill bottles all around her. The nurse said that this was no place for a teenage boy, but the Sick Lady shooed the cranky woman out of the room and pointed to the chair next to the bed. The Girl Who Would Choose Her Own Name sat down and promised herself that she wasn't going to cry.

"I see you," the Sick Lady said.

"I see you because I was you. I wish I could make it easier. But I'm not going to start lying just because I'm making my final exit. You will always be who you once were and you will spend the rest of your life trying to figure out who you are now. Looking for yourself will keep you brave. It will show you strengths unimaginable."

In her will, the Sick Lady left the Girl Who Would Choose Her Own Name a bank account she couldn't touch until she turned twenty-five, her collection of costume jewelry, and the posters that had hung on her dressing room walls at Café le Rouge. The Sick Lady once called the jewelry and posters "priceless," and without price they remained. Not even when the Girl Who Would Choose Her Own Name went through a really bad time, not even then, did she sell her gifts.

Eventually, the Girl Who Would Choose Her Own Name got her head on straight. And when she did, she realized that she could not stay in the City if she was to become who she was. She left the apartment with Avó yelling condemnations and Mãe weeping tears of heartbreak and understanding.

Once she was on her own, the Girl Who Would Choose Her Own Name decided she needed a new name for her new self.

The one she picked, it meant "reborn."

THE WAREHOUSE OF
DANCERS AND DREAMERS

SID WAS STILL IN THE shower when the first of Renata's friends arrived. The curtain hid him, but his singing rang loud and clear from the back corner to the front door.

> *"Oh. Oh. Oh. Mmmmmm.*
> *For one more night I'm in your heart. . . ."*

The bearded guy held up a six-pack of beer and tiptoed into the kitchen, while the woman in a metallic green jacket who had come in with him hugged Renata. When the woman broke free, she pressed a finger to her lips, stepped out of her heeled boots, and tiptoed across the warehouse floor.

"That's Katie," Renata whispered to Homer, Mia, and Einstein. They'd all drifted into the kitchen area after the doorbell rang. "We sing at the same club three nights a week. Voice like an angel." Renata made a zipper motion across her lips and they all turned to watch.

> *"Da. Da. Da. Do. Do. Do.*
> *And you're the whole of mine.*
> *Oh. Oh. Mmmmmm."*

Then, "Hey, Einstein," Sid shouted, bringing Katie to a halt about a foot from the bathtub. "What's the next—"

> *"But till then, we party like rock stars—"*

Katie's voice was low and smoky.

Sid's shriek, however, was high enough to shatter glass. "Oh. My. God. Are people here? Do they know I'm naked?" A bar of soap thumped on the side of the tub, then slid across the floor, followed by the water shutting off and more shouting. "I'm going to kill you guys! Not Mia, but—"

> *"And I'll keep your hand in mine . . ."*

Katie kept on singing as she turned and bowed.

> *"'Cause tonight's the last song of our lives.*
> *Oh, tonight's the very last song of our lives."*

The shower curtain billowed as Sid scrambled around inside. "Whoever's singing out there, I think I'm in love with you. But—" He flung open the curtain. He had a faded blue towel wrapped around his waist and streaks of soap across his skinny chest. "A gentleman puts on pants before singing a duet."

Katie started laughing so hard she had to clutch her stomach with one hand while offering Sid the other, which he gallantly accepted as he stepped out of the tub.

The doorbell rang again just moments after Sid shut the bathroom door behind him. The DJ had arrived. After that, the guests kept pouring in, glittering wave after glittering wave.

A couple of hours in, Homer was grateful to find a spot to lean against. He settled on the arm of the tire-mark sofa, sighed, sipped the fruity drink Katie had made him, and watched the shimmering crowd. Homer knew he was the opposite of a chatty, cool-at-parties person, but Renata had introduced him to practically everyone who'd come through the door and he'd found himself standing with strangers in circles and talking to them as if he went to parties like this all the time on Wednesday nights.

How am I going to describe this to anyone back home? Homer wondered as two women, one in boots that laced up to her knees and the other in an elaborate dress the color of grape cold medicine, walked by. *I won't get it right, but Mia will. She'll be able to tell the stories.* The thought made Homer start to smile, but then he remembered. *Mia could tell the stories, but she won't be there. After tomorrow, she's gone.*

He'd gotten so caught up in the trip that he'd let why they were driving in the first place hide behind the Now Happenings, the Present, the Right-This-Moment-No-Thoughts-About-Tomorrow. *Maybe there's still time. Maybe I can still change her mind.* Homer took a gulp of Katie's drink, grimaced at the aftertaste, and willed his brain to shut down. *Just for one more night. Just one more night off from thinking.* He focused on people watching instead.

The crowd was unlike any other Homer had ever been a part of. Most of Renata's friends were like her: singers, artists, and performers. Their outfits had sequins. Their high heels were super tall. Their hairdos eccentric. Each person Homer talked to was working toward something spectacular, grand, world-changing, mind-bending, or—his favorite description—life-altering.

To listen to them, you'd think that without a doubt they were *all* destined to be the next big thing. They were *all* geniuses and unrecognized talents of unknowable proportions. They were stars waiting in the wings, celebrities tapping their toes for their turns in the spotlight.

Even if some of them don't make it, Homer thought, as he sipped his sweet but burning drink, *at least they'll know they wanted something.*

Renata caught Homer's eye as he was watching two women,

both brunettes, and both would-be dancers by all appearances, compete to see who could spin the fastest without spilling her drink. By the time Renata had made her way to Homer, a winner had been declared. The shorter brunette hadn't wasted a drop of whatever was in her red plastic cup. In response to the decision, her opponent threw back her head, finishing whatever was left in her cup, and conceded defeat with a wobbling curtsy.

"We are all rock stars and prizewinners here. Poets and activists. Waiters and baristas, all meant for grander things." Renata motioned for the guy Homer had been trying not to elbow to move over, which he did, and she leaned next to Homer, against the armrest of the couch. "It's a beautiful desperation, really, to need to believe, to actually believe, that it's right there, just on the horizon, and it will be ours someday."

"What will be yours?" Homer tried to turn his head so he could see Renata's expression, but that would mean bracing one arm behind the guy Renata had moved. So he continued looking forward, watching the many performances popping up throughout the crowd like bubbles rising in a fizzy drink. A guy who had to be older than Homer's dads was demonstrating yo-yo tricks to a group by the door. The taller dancer who'd lost the spinning contest was now showing a guy in tight jeans and a fedora how she could slide into a split. Someone juggled fruit in the kitchen while someone else by the windows sang the chorus of an old show tune.

Renata didn't reply. She was quiet for the length of a long

exhale, enough time for the DJ to change from a jazzy oldie to a mash-up of the Apollo Aces song Sid had been singing earlier and a hip-hop song that'd been popular when Homer was a sophomore. The room erupted, bodies scurried to the makeshift dance floor, jumping, spinning, dipping, and twisting, shouting the chorus like they wanted all of Hopeville to know they were here.

Homer shook his head. "Why does everyone love Apollo Aces?"

"I don't know about everyone, but Sid definitely does," Renata said, pointing to the far corner of the dance floor, where Sid seemed to be trying to shake every part of his body simultaneously. Einstein, dancing next to him, was lost in his own groove, as was Poncho, who was swaying side to side languidly behind them. "Looks like he's having a terrible time." Renata underscored her irony with a smile.

"Sid's not going to want to go back to his old life." Homer laughed. "And Einstein can dance? Wow. He might not want to go back either." Homer watched his little brother trying to teach Sid how to bounce in rhythm before he spoke again. "Thank you again, by the way. You don't really have any—"

"It's passing along a kindness," Renata interrupted. "You say 'thank you' one more time, I'll turn red, and embarrassment does not look good on me. Understand?"

Homer pressed his lips together and nodded.

Renata sighed happily. "Did you know, there are eighty

thousand people in this city? That's eighty thousand stories to tell and hear and each of them as different from the other as one snowflake from the next." She tipped sideways suddenly, putting an arm on Homer's wrist for balance. "Phew. Thank you, darling. I told Rudolph not to be so damn cheap, but he always gets this terrible plastic-bottle rum. Gets me drunker than a skunk. Renders me utterly useless in the morning." She shook her cup and took a deep drink. "What were we talking about?"

"Um . . ." Homer's voice trailed off when he saw Mia in the corner by the windows. She was sitting in one of the beanbag chairs among a small group of guys so oddly dressed that they had to be either musicians or performance artists. When Mia noticed Homer looking at her, she tilted her head to the side. "Okay?" She moved her mouth with careful exaggeration, giving each silent syllable its own moment across her lips.

"Okay," Homer replied in turn, mimicking her deliberate movements.

Renata pushed against Homer's forearm to get to her feet. When she wobbled, he jumped up and caught her elbow. Once she was steady, Renata looked knowingly at Homer over the top of her drink; the fake eyelashes she had methodically reapplied hours earlier were long enough to graze her cheeks when she blinked. She raised her cup as if she were making a toast. "To love—that indomitable urge, that leap into the abyss." She slid an arm around Homer's shoulders and turned him so they were both looking at the dance floor. "Look at those beautiful stargazers. Each and every one of them dreaming a separate dream, but all hoping for the same thing."

"Love?" Homer asked.

"Yes. Love. The greatest man-made disaster in a world that's full of them." Renata squeezed Homer's shoulder and shifted so her back was to the crowd and she was looking straight at him. "Poets say love is forever. Country singers, that it's something you drown in beer and cheap whiskey. Meanwhile, the men in white coats blame love on hormones, evolution, and chemicals in our brains. You could ask every person here what love is, and you'd get a different answer each time." Renata sighed. For no longer than a heartbeat, the smile on her bright-pink lips didn't match the feeling in her dark-brown eyes.

"But I think you're doing just fine coming up with your own understanding," she added. "I've monopolized you enough. Go. Rescue your lady before they start strumming those guitars. Sweet boys, but between the five of them, they couldn't play a kazoo."

Renata turned and started to walk toward the dance floor. "Take her to the park on the river," she called over her shoulder. "This time of night, there's always an officer camped out. Safest place in Hopeville." Renata handed her cup to a guy with dreadlocks, who took it without protest. Then she disappeared into the crush of dreamers, all of them dancing with abandon because they needed to lose themselves—if only for the length of a song—in something other than their dreams.

It took ten minutes of conversation about four-string versus five-string guitars before Homer was able to rescue Mia from the circle of aspiring musicians. It took three more for them to make their way to the corner behind the bathtub where they'd stashed their coats and bags, and an additional forty-five seconds to weave between the dancing bodies to the exit.

"Sweet molasses! This feels good," Mia shouted as soon as she stepped out into the street. "It's hot in there." Her coat flapped like a half-opened parachute as she half ran, half skipped around the side of Renata's building, calling, "Watch out for the glass!" just before she disappeared from Homer's sight.

After a beat, Homer followed her, stepping over the broken glass that trailed from the street into the park they'd seen through Renata's window. Mia was already leaning against the metal railing that overlooked the river by the time he caught up.

"Look at the water. It's like a whole other city is down there—a softer one." Mia stepped onto the railing's bottom rung, which was just high enough to make Homer nervous. He moved closer, ready to catch her if he needed to.

Only once Mia straightened did Homer allow himself to look down. She was right. There was a second city floating on top of the black, slow-moving water. The lights coming from all the bright apartment windows on land were dazzling, but their reflections were muted, the sharpness of the buildings hazy. Even the river's smell was subdued, brackish instead of oily, soil and decaying leaves instead of pavement and rubber. It was nothing like the turquoise water of La Isla de Plátanos, but it wasn't bad—just different.

"When I was in the first place with Dotts, there was a small creek behind the house." Mia stepped down from the railing. "She and I would go back there and pretend it was a river. She was obsessed with boats, so we'd imagine that a big one was going to come chugging along and it'd stop and we'd get on and go wherever it took us." Mia bit her lip and smiled, but it was a wistful smile, equal parts longing and loss.

When Homer leaned next to her, Mia slid her arms across the railing, until her side was touching his: shoulder to shoulder, elbow to elbow, hip to hip. She reached for his hand and slid both their hands into Homer's coat pocket. "Your coat is bigger than mine. That means you've got more room to share."

"I'm a big guy." Homer swallowed. Now was as good a time as any to bring up the future. "When was the last time you saw Dotts?"

"Hmmm." Mia shifted from one foot to the other. "Two years ago. She wasn't in Glory-Be, yet. I remember because I'd just gotten my out-and-out check—"

"Out and out?" It was just cold enough for Homer's words to turn into puffs of white.

"When you turn eighteen, you age out of the foster system and you're out on your own, but the government gives you a check to get you started. Dotts and I and the others called them 'out-and-outs.'"

Mia could easily have listed her favorite foods or talked about the temperature with the same tone that she used to explain her life. No self-pity. No anger. Homer wanted to wrap his arms around her, but also didn't want her to stop talking. He settled for squeezing her hand instead.

"Look!" Mia pointed into the dark.

Homer followed the invisible line from the tip of Mia's finger to the gray shadow of a tugboat moving up the river against the current. Its steady *chug, chug, chug* was comforting. The other night sounds—horns honking, music ringing from open windows, shrieking tires on the bridge—seemed sharper, louder, in its wake.

Homer waited for the wail of a siren to fade before he spoke. "Can I ask you something?"

"Fire away."

"How are you so *you* all the time?" Homer took a deep breath. "I mean, you haven't exactly had it easy. Like, I would probably hate my mom if she did what yours did. You have all these reasons to be mad at the universe, but you're not."

Mia let go of Homer's hand and folded her arms over the railing. She didn't respond for so long that Homer was opening his mouth to apologize when she spoke. "She did the best she could, I think. She didn't have a great life. Like, she really loved my dad. And then he left and she just wanted the pain to go away." Mia turned her head to look up at Homer. "She tried rehab—a few times. But it didn't work."

Homer twisted his hands back and forth over the top railing, ignoring the bite of the cold metal. "I guess what I'm asking is, How are you so happy? Your everyday attitude is ten times more upbeat than the tourists who come into the shop, and those are people on vacation."

The nearest streetlight buzzed loudly, then went dark, leaving Mia's face half lit as she answered. "I don't know. Part of it was me realizing that people like happy kids more. If you're nice you stick out, but in a good way. People treat you better. They let you stay longer. The other part is probably just me. Just Mia. It's the way I am."

"Who's 'they'?"

"What?"

"When you said 'they let you stay longer,' who did you mean by 'they'?"

"Foster parents, people who might want to adopt you, yada yada yada." Mia made a dismissive motion with her hand.

Homer pressed his chest against the railing. "Yeah. That makes sense." It didn't, but he wasn't sure what else to say.

"Now you have to tell me something."

"Okay."

"What's the *real* worst thing you've ever done? I don't buy the towel story. Not even from Mr. Nice Guy Finn."

Homer stared at the water, trying to look like he was thinking of an answer.

"Earth to Homer."

"It's more like something that I didn't do." Homer took Mia's silence as an encouragement to continue. "When I was a sophomore, I went through this thing where I wanted to try out a bunch of religions. Weird, I know."

"I've heard stranger."

Homer smiled. "So one day, my friend Travis convinced me to come to his youth group. He's probably my best friend at school. A great guy, like help-old-ladies-cross-the-street great, so I went. And at first, it was fine. Just a lot of talk about community service schedules and winter break. But then this moron I've known since kindergarten, Tom Witherspoon, he gets up and starts saying stuff about needing to be 'more proactive,' and 'moral values,' and a bunch of other crap. Sorry, Tadpole."

Mia nudged Homer's shoulder. "Keep going."

"Tom, who was wearing pleated khakis, by the way, like he was seventy instead of sixteen, worked himself up into a rant about 'perversion' and the 'homosexual agenda,' and suddenly I noticed that everyone was looking anywhere else but in my direction—including Travis. And even then, it took me another minute to get it."

"Get what?" Mia's hair drifted over her face as she leaned toward Homer.

Homer closed his eyes. "That this jerk was saying terrible stuff about gay people, about people like my dads. That he was standing there basically vomiting hate and he didn't care who heard him."

"That's—"

"But the worst thing is, I just sat there. Like an idiot. I sat there for the rest of the meeting like a big, dumb rock. I could have said something at any point. I could have turned over a desk, broken some chalk, but I didn't even leave. I. Just. Sat. There."

"Homer, I'm sorry. So many people—"

"You would have said something. Einstein would have quoted some scholar or the Bible to totally prove Tom wrong."

"I would have cried. I'm a crier."

Homer coughed. "At least you would have reacted."

"What happened after? After the meeting?"

"I picked up my bag and walked out. I saw Travis following me. I knew he was going to apologize or try to explain, but I didn't want to hear him, so I practically ran away. Every time he brought it up for the next week, I changed the subject. Not because I was mad at him, but because I was so mad at myself."

"Guess you didn't join the group."

"Ha." Homer's attempt at a laugh sounded like he had a pill stuck in his throat. "I took a break from all extracurriculars for a while. I tried a few more clubs a couple months later, went to synagogue with one of D.B.'s friends when he was visiting, but it wasn't the same."

"What do you mean?"

"It wasn't just that I didn't believe in anything, it was that I didn't believe I could believe. Does that make sense?"

"Actually, it does." Mia rubbed her stomach. Her voice sounded saturated. Even though she whispered, the words were heavy. "It makes a lot of sense." Mia paused. "Homer, would you do me a favor?"

"Let me guess, ice-cream run."

"Close your eyes."

"Uh, why?"

"Because I want to kiss you, and if you have your eyes open, I'm afraid I'm going to chicken out."

Homer wiped his hands against his pants. Ducked his head. Looked at the river. Wished he could scrub his face against his sleeve or check his breath against his palm.

"Please."

It was the way she said "please," like the one word was both a demand and a question. So he did. Homer closed his eyes.

He expected her lips on his, but that wasn't what happened. First, Homer felt her breath on his neck, right below his left ear. A warm whisper against his cold skin. Then he felt her lips pressed to the very same spot, making him shiver in the way that only goose bumps can. He felt his hip bump against the railing, but just barely. Her lips left a trail of fruity gloss as she gently kissed Homer's jaw, left to right, and then finally put her mouth to his.

Kissing her was not like anything he could have imagined.

The first time they broke apart, Mia rested against Homer's chest, her hair tickling his nose. The second time they kissed,

Homer opened his eyes, just for a moment. The third time, they only stopped kissing because the police officer Renata had promised would be guarding the park yelled at them to get inside.

So they did. Holding hands and laughing as they danced over the path of broken glass and out of the night.

They fell asleep side by side on one of the twin mattresses Renata had distributed across her apartment floor. And even though he was terrified about bumping Tadpole and morning breath and a million other things, Homer fell asleep holding Mia's hand.

That was all. That was everything.

THE CAR OF CELESTIAL STINK AND THE TOWN OF UNEXPECTED EVERYTHING

WHEN HOMER WOKE UP THE next morning, his first thought wasn't to wonder where he was or how someone had painted a pattern of swirls and circles on Renata's ceiling. His first thought was that today was the day they'd reach Glory-Be and he'd say good-bye to Mia. His second thought was an extension of the first. *How has anyone ever, in the whole history of the universe, survived a broken heart?*

As Poncho had promised, Martha was very hungover and a very good mechanic. She had already been tinkering under the Banana's hood for hours when Homer and Einstein stumbled out of Renata's building to hunt down coffee, bagels, and the vitamin C tablets Renata swore were the only way to counteract too much cheap rum.

By a little after eleven, Martha slammed down the hood. It was the strangest engine she'd ever worked on, she said, but it was fixed.

Poncho shook their hands and Renata gave them all hugs and accused them of making her puffy-eyed. And then Mia was behind the wheel, Homer in the passenger seat, and Einstein and Sid were in the back, comparing notes from the party and each trying to outdo the other with "cools" and "awesomes."

Two hours into the long drive from one end of Massachusetts to the other, Homer couldn't ignore the smell any longer. And even though the DJ for whatever station Mia had chosen promised that it was "a cold one out there," Homer cranked down his window and tried to inhale as much fresh air as he could.

"Shut the window. It's freezing," Einstein yelled from the backseat. With his sweatshirt hood pulled up and his glasses askew, he looked like an angry owl.

"It's kind of fun," Sid said, leaning over Einstein. "Hey, do you think this is what it's like to be inside a freezer with a fan?"

Homer took a final deep breath of air scented with frozen dirt and grass. He'd started to roll the window back up when the smell struck again. "Aww, Steiner, I know you're lactose intolerant, but that's just rude. Major S.F."

"I didn't fart."

Homer pulled his shirt over his nose, so his voice was muffled. "Sure."

"Maybe we ran over a skunk," Einstein said before he ducked his nose into his sweatshirt. He looked even more like a grumpy bird.

"Homer, the car's smelled terrible for days." Mia swallowed like she was trying not to laugh. "How have you not noticed until now?" She turned her eyes back to the road as she passed a tractor trailer and a large SUV.

"See?" said Einstein, his voice muffled by his sweatshirt. "Even *I* know not to fart in a closed environment."

"It has?" Homer took his nose out of his shirt.

"It smelled like a combination of rotten fruit and burned coffee when I got in here." Sid stuck his face between the two front seats. "And it's gotten worse every day since. Maybe you did run over a skunk and it's stuck in the engine?" he added helpfully.

"It's not skunk," Mia said as she flipped through the radio stations. "It's like its own powerful, disgusting combination."

"Yeah." Einstein kicked the back of Homer's seat as he sat up. "It's pineapple mixed with old leather and stale chips."

"Whose fault are the stale chips?" Homer called over his shoulder.

"Don't look at me," Einstein replied indignantly. "I'm not the one who didn't know chips were crumbly."

"In my defense," Sid said, raising his pointer finger, "I had never had chips before."

"It's more like a swamp that's been sprinkled with powdered sugar and put under a heat lamp," Mia said.

"Good one." Einstein nodded.

"Dirty sneakers left in a locker room with a broken thermostat," Homer said.

"This car smells like an outhouse," Sid chimed.

"Lame," Einstein responded. "How about . . ."

The game went on for the next thirty minutes or so, but Homer stopped noticing the smell—or, really, much of anything else—when Mia reached across the console and rested her hand on top of his. Her simple gesture, the feeling of her hand on his, was just enough to remind him where they were going and what he was losing.

The closer they got to Glory-Be-by-the-Sea, the quieter Mia became and the slower traffic went. When Homer said something about how weird it was that Route 16 was this backed up in December, she nodded, but that was it.

Mia drove and Homer reminded himself to breathe. When he tried to pull his thoughts together into what he wanted to say, his mind became a bunch of rocks scudding down a mountain and his heart felt more and more like a waterlogged stuffed toy. Outside the Banana, horns honked and music thumped through car radios, but inside, Einstein and Sid snuffled and snored in the back and the cracked leather of the passenger seat sighed as Homer shifted so he could rest his arm on top of the empty cupholders and hold Mia's hand. Without looking over, without taking her eyes from the road, she turned her wrist so she could weave her fingers through his, and she pulled his hand to her cheek.

When she lowered her arm, she sighed but didn't let go of

his hand. Not even when they drove by a large, faded billboard that declared in bold black letters "Congratulations! You've Reached Glory-Be-by-the-Sea!" and Homer managed to not choke on the directions he didn't want to give, for Mia to take the next left turn. Not even then did she let go.

If it hadn't been for the crowd of people streaming over the sidewalks and streets like a massive school of fish, Glory-Be-by-the-Sea would have been the epitome of a resort town in winter. *Any other day*, Homer thought, *this place might be pretty*.

The beach dunes looked crystallized, like handfuls of sugar had been tossed on top of the sand. Thin patches of snow hid in shadowed corners and other protected places like hibernating animals. Most business windows were covered with plywood, the stores' flagpoles naked, the signs on the doors all turned to show the "Closed" side.

Mia drove by three parking lots before she found one that had spaces left. She was reaching to hand money to the parking-lot attendant, an old guy in overalls and flannel, when Einstein poked his head between the front seats.

"Sir. What's going on? Why are all these people here?" He sounded like he was still waking up.

The attendant shuffled Mia's bill into the roll he had pulled from one of his many pockets. He tipped his cap up, licked a finger, and counted off three one-dollar bills and handed them to Mia. "New thing they're testing at the Salvation Ballroom. Having a winter concert series. Trying to keep the money rolling in year-round." He spoke each word deliberately, like he didn't want to waste a single one on explanations.

"Who's performing?" Sid tried to shove his face next to Einstein's, but gave up when Einstein wouldn't move over.

"Guy called Apollo Aces." The old man shrugged. "Not my cuppa, but show's been sold out for months. You kids fans?" He pulled his hat brim down before bending so his face was even with the window. "'Cause if you are, I might be able to get my hands on some tickets. There's a courtesy charge, of course. Something along the lines of—"

"Yes!" This time Einstein let himself be pushed back so Sid could lean into the front. "How much for four tickets?"

"Two." Homer cleared his throat. "You two should go. I'll help Mia with her stuff . . . and stuff." He would have smacked his forehead if he could've without calling more attention to his lameness.

"Awesome," Sid said, falling into the backseat just long enough to dig money out of his backpack before he shoved himself between the front seats again. "Is two hundred dollars enough?" Sid reached over Mia and held two crisp bills out the driver's-side window.

"You raised beneath a rock, kid?" the parking-lot attendant asked as he snatched the bills with one hand while the other grabbed two tickets from his coat pocket. "You can't wave money around like that. Here." He handed Sid the tickets and pointed vaguely to the lot behind him.

"Thank you," Sid said as he slid into his seat. He and Einstein stared at the slips of paper like they couldn't believe they were real while Mia rolled up her window. "This is the coolest."

It took some circling around for Mia to find an empty space large enough to fit the Banana, but less than one minute to decide on the plan: Homer and Mia would walk to Dotts's place. Einstein and Sid would follow the crowd to the Salvation Ballroom. They'd meet back at the car after the concert to say good-bye to Mia.

At the parking-lot entrance, Einstein and Sid turned right and were soon caught up in the flow of people. Homer and Mia turned left and walked against the current of excited concert-goers. Mia reached for Homer's hand and he let himself be pulled behind her.

After a few minutes of following, Homer knew when Mia was going to turn left and when she was going to turn right almost at the same time she did. The farther they got away from downtown, the narrower the streets became, and the closer the tiny houses with neat yards, picket fences, and tidy white trim grew together.

At the turn for Seahorse Street, Homer promised himself, *I'll say something by the house with the red mailbox. Definitely, by the final house.* But as they shuffled onto Blueberry Lane, Homer felt like he would choke on everything he wanted to say but couldn't.

Okay. If a car passes by before the end, I have to say something. I need to say something. A white van with rusted doors and "Henry's Finest Seafood" across the side rolled by, so Homer cleared his throat. "Mia?"

He must not have spoken loudly enough, because Mia turned onto Ocean Avenue and stopped at the second house on the right side of the street. Only after she started pushing the gate—which stuck against the uneven path like it too was protesting her decision—did Mia look up.

"Ready?"

Homer wasn't, but he nodded anyway, dropped Mia's hand, and then walked up and rang the bell, reciting *Let nobody be home. Let nobody be home.* in his head like an incantation.

The door opened immediately. "Hello. You here about the apartment?" The woman who stood behind the screen door was tall and pretty, though obviously exhausted. She had purple smudges under her eyes and she leaned against the doorknob like she needed help to stay upright. The only parts of her of that didn't look life-weary were her eyes, which were a startling blue. Two slices of sea glass resting in afternoon-lit sand.

"Sorry," the woman said, looking at the delicate watch looped on her left wrist. "I am so late for the afternoon shift, and I've still got to get the baby up from his nap. If you're interested in the apartment and don't mind me shouting at you as I run around, come in."

"We're—" The women let the screen door slam shut behind her before Homer could continue. He turned around. Mia had drifted down the cracked walkway to the place where the sidewalk met the winter-brown front lawn. Her arms were wrapped around her stomach. She looked so alone, it made something catch in Homer's chest. His breath felt studded with thorns.

"Mia." Her name came out a whisper; it could not possibly reach her. Homer cleared his throat. "Mia." Her hair lifted and fell in fruit-punch-red waves, but no other part of her moved.

The third time, Homer shouted her name, surprising himself with how scared he sounded. "Mia." This time she turned. "She invited us in." Homer gestured toward the door.

Mia's arms hung by her sides like invisible cinder blocks were attached to her wrists as she made her way up the path. "Sure," she said, ducking under Homer's arm to go through the doorway. "Let's."

Homer followed her in, gently pulling the door shut behind him. He wanted to ask, "Where's Dotts?" but he caught the words and turned them into a cough before he could. He wasn't exactly sure why.

It took a moment for his eyes to adjust to the dim light. The door opened up right into a living room with a small flatscreen TV, a plaid love seat, and wall-to-wall carpeting littered with baby toys.

The woman with the shockingly blue eyes appeared in the doorway of the kitchen at the end of the hall. A baby, wearing only a diaper, rested on one of her hips, a waffle clutched in its two hands.

As she walked toward them, Homer saw that she had changed into an all-black outfit and pulled her hair into ponytail at the nape of her neck.

"Sorry about that. Goober here," she said, touching her forehead against the baby's, "is teething and doesn't give his poor mommy a moment's rest. Do you?" The pitch of her voice rose as she made cooing sounds. The baby pumped the waffle up and down, banging the woman on the nose and flinging crumbs on her face. "Motherhood is so glamorous," she said, wiping her cheek against her shoulder. "But I guess you'll find that out soon enough." She jutted her chin toward Mia, who hadn't moved far from the door. "When are you due?"

"February," Mia croaked. "I call mine Tadpole." Her voice made the barbs in Homer's chest catch again.

"Good name. Goober's daddy, piece of shit that he is, used to call him Guppy, but we changed that to Goober when Mommy kicked his ass to the curb. Didn't we, sweetheart. We sure did." The woman straightened up. "So I can't let you see the space now. My brother's repainting it and the fumes are terrible, but it'll be ready at the end of the month. It's just over the garage. It's what you'd call cozy." She looked Homer up and down. "You might have to duck in some places, but it has a good-size kitchen, window in the bathroom, and built-in closets. If you can survive living there with a newborn, you two will make it much longer than me and my ex."

"Oh, we're not," Mia stammered. "Tadpole's not Homer's."

"We're not here about the apartment," Homer said, just a beat after Mia. "Sorry. I'm—"

"You here for a cut? I don't work out of the house anymore." The woman dragged a bulging black purse from under a side table and starting sifting through it with the hand that wasn't holding the baby. "I rent a booth at Orleans Beauty and Spa on East Main. Had to get out of the house or— Why can't I ever find anything in here? There they are." She dropped the purse and handed a business card to Homer, then another to Mia, who took the cardboard rectangle and held it listlessly in front of her, dangling it between two fingers. "Since you're new customers, I can count one of you as a referral. Ten percent off." The woman tilted her head as she studied Mia. "Can't do much about your roots while you're expecting. But a rinse might even out the color some until you can dye it again."

"Trisha Moore. Licensed Esthetician." Homer read out loud without knowing if he meant to. The connection between his head and the rest of him was scrambled, hazy. "Sorry. I . . . I think we got the wrong house. Do you know Dotts, I mean Dorothy Sampson?"

"You two her friends?" Trisha asked, but didn't wait for an answer. "Wow. That girl did *not* tell anyone she was leaving, did she?" Trisha wiped waffle crumbs off her arm as she spoke. "I wish I could tell you some good news, but Dorothy ran out on a month's rent three or so months ago. I haven't seen her since. She seemed like a good kid who'd been knocked around by life and bad luck. I felt for her, you know." Trisha kissed the top of the baby's head.

Mia didn't say anything, so neither did Homer. They must have looked disappointed, or maybe Trisha just felt compelled to fill the silence, because she added, "She, Dorothy, was doing real good for a while. I got her a job as a shampoo girl. She was going to school at night. All that." Trisha swung her hips from side to side, cooing to Goober before adding, "Didn't help that she was hooking up with a lowlife from Varney Beach. Whatever reason she ran off for, I bet that SOB's behind it."

Trisha looked at her watch. "Shit. I'm sorry, but I've got to go." She scooped her purse off the floor and flung it over her left shoulder and smiled at them apologetically as she held the door for Mia, then Homer, before shutting and locking it.

Homer watched her put Goober in a car seat in the white SUV parked on a driveway of broken shells and white stones. When Trisha waved as she backed into the street, Homer waved back automatically. His mouth puffed frozen ghost words into the air. "Thank you."

Only then did he turn his head to find Mia already standing on the sidewalk. Only then did he realize how the orange in the funny ball on the top of her winter hat looked really cute with her red hair. Only then did he see that the afternoon had clouded over while they were inside—or maybe it had been overcast before, but he'd been too wrapped up in thinking of all the things he wasn't brave enough to say to notice.

It didn't matter. What mattered was that the sky had gone gray. Mia looked more lost than Homer knew a person could be. And it was cold and December and beginning to snow.

THE PARABLE OF THE GIRL
WHO COULD BREAK

THE GIRL WHO COULD BREAK liked to discover animals in the clouds and words in the sand. She looked for famous faces in burned toast and patterns in cracked concrete. She had started the game right after the first time her world fell apart and she'd kept playing it through every time since.

The Girl Who Could Break found it comforting to spot recognizable things when she was thrown into otherwise unrecognizable new lives, to uncover something known in the unknown, to have control amid chaos and order where there seemed to be none. She recited aphorisms and clichés like she believed them—because she did.

ALL CLOUDS HAVE A SILVER LINING.
IT'S BETTER TO HAVE LOVED AND LOST THAN
NEVER TO HAVE LOVED AT ALL.

KEEP YOUR CHIN UP, BECAUSE THERE'S NO USE

CRYING OVER SPILLED MILK.

AND THAT WHICH DOES NOT KILL YOU MAKES

YOU STRONGER.

SO LET YOUR HAIR DOWN AND WEAR YOUR

HEART ON YOUR SLEEVE.

PUT YOUR BEST FOOT FORWARD WHILE

STANDING AND DELIVERING.

But like any system here on this imperfect third planet from the sun, the one that the Girl Who Could Break created could (and did) falter.

It turns out to be a beautiful illusion, she discovered, that forces beyond her reach were actually within it.

It turns out that the tea leaves aren't symbols. They're just the scraps some person chose to leave behind.

It turns out that she was an idiot to believe that good things happen to good people and bad things to bad.

She was a fool to have told herself for so long that the next sunrise would be brighter and tomorrow would, indeed, be another, better, day.

There are only so many disappointments a person can take before her faith begins to show the cracks in the facade. There is only so much a person can endure before she realizes that the proverbial lemonade she is supposed to make with her life's metaphorical lemons is just sour juice with too much sugar.

THE BEACH OF SAND AND SNOW

WHEN TRISHA'S CAR DISAPPEARED around the corner, Mia started walking, and Homer followed her all the way to the beach and then right up to the water's edge.

Homer had never seen a beach in the cold. It looked like a place from another planet. The water was a navy blue so dark it was almost black. The white froth of the waves looked sculpted. Frost made the stalks of sea grass on the dunes shimmer, and when snowflakes landed on the dense sand, they only lingered for a heartbeat before getting sucked beneath the surface. It didn't smell like a beach. Maybe the salt was trapped beneath the frozen rocks. Maybe, come spring, the stench of rotting seaweed would take over, just as soon as the sun remembered what it was meant to do.

The air was uneven, some breezes warmer than others. *Because of the Gulf Stream*, Homer thought as he watched the blue-black waves pick away the sand from around the smooth gray rock at his feet. *Or is it because of the way the cold in the sky interacts with the cold in the water? Einstein will know. I'll ask him when we start driving again.* Homer reached down and worked the rock free from the sand. It was much larger than he'd thought it would be, and though he threw as hard as he could, it plunked into the water only a few yards from the shore. *Do we keep with the plan? Go to New Hampshire? What happens after you get to where you were supposed to be and it ends up not being the supposed-to-be place at all?*

"Homer."

Homer heard Mia but didn't. It was like she was calling him from the shore and he was trying to make sense of the world on the beach from a world underwater. The only thing that was clear to him at that moment was that miles and months after the Anywhere Girl walked into La Isla Souvenirs, she was still a mystery.

"Homer."

A snowflake landed on the end of his nose. Homer crossed his eyes and watched it melt. His nose and fingers felt cold, but his cheeks were warm. Maybe he'd gotten sunburned and hadn't noticed. Or maybe the northern wind was roughing up his delicate Florida skin. Maybe he wasn't cut out for the cold or living anywhere other than La Isla de Plátanos.

The wish that he had never left, that he was home or at school or even at the store doing inventory hit him like a rubber band snapping. Homer had to think about breathing in and out, and then Mia was standing next to him, strands of her fruit-punch hair sticking to her face, obscuring her eyes. *Is she crying or is snow melting on her face, too?*

"I think I missed something. Or maybe I was too oblivious to understand." Homer cleared his throat. "Where's Dotts? Didn't she know you were coming?"

Mia shook her head. "I didn't want—" She was speaking so softly that the wind picked apart her words. "I needed to hope."

Homer wiped his face on his sleeve. "Sorry?"

"I needed to hope that Dotts would be here. That's how it works," Mia said slowly. "When it's just me, it doesn't matter how it turns out. I pick a new postcard . . . and . . . I really, really wanted her to be here. She said she loved it. That's what the postcard says on the back. She loved it and would never leave and I should come and live with her, and it'd be just like before."

Homer pulled his hat down, once, twice on each side. He didn't know where to look. The water was too black and too endless and it made him feel too small and unimportant. The sand, frozen and hard, confused him. Sand wasn't supposed to be that way. And Mia—looking at Mia was impossible, not if he wanted to stay upright, not if he couldn't handle more of him falling apart.

Homer nudged a shell out of the sand with the tip of his right sneaker, then turned his foot and kicked it. The shell barely moved, but sand went flying into the wind.

"Oh."

"Oh God. I'm sorry." Before he realized what he was doing, Homer brushed a blob of sand off Mia's coat, "Your eyes are red. Did it hit your face?"

"No." Mia sniffed. Strands of her hair stuck to her cheeks.

Homer raised his hand, then lowered it. Shoved both hands in his coat pockets.

Mia's hands were pink with cold, but she kept them hanging by her sides. "This is the first time that it's not just me. I'm sorry. I was greedy. I wanted too much. I wanted you to come with me . . . to . . . to not go alone just this one time."

"Doesn't it get exhausting? Always running away? Or maybe you're running *to* places. I don't know." Homer was surprised at how aloof he sounded. He wasn't certain he meant to. "Pinning all your hopes on geography. Each time, you get to pretend that the shitty stuff won't follow you and that it's better for the people you're leaving. Is that how it works?"

"You make it sound like I don't care about hurting you." Mia's words rattled and clicked. "I told you I'm not a good person. I'm not sweet. I'm not pretty. You just feel bad for me because I'm so stupid and 'cause I'm knocked up. And I'm going to mess up just like everyone messed up before me, because that's who I am."

"Who?" Homer ran his tongue over his lips. They were chapped. Bits of skin came off. *Disgusting.* "Who is 'everyone'?" Homer's voice cracked. He didn't care. As long as the stinging in his eyes was from the cold and not the start of tears. "I just want to understand what the hell you're saying. I need to comprehend how big a moron I am."

"You're not a moron, Homer," Mia said, shaking her head. "I am." She sniffled. Wiped her nose. Continued. "I actually thought that if I wasn't like the other kids, if I was sweet and polite and smiled a lot, they wouldn't care that I was dumb or that my own mom didn't want me. And maybe one of them would adopt me." Mia's gaze went from the ground to the black water and back to the ground again. "I didn't ask for you to fall in love with me. I didn't want you to."

"What do you mean? You can't require a permission slip. People fall in love. It's not something you control."

"I don't know what I mean anymore." Mia shook her head side to side. The wind whipped her hair in all directions, but if it stung her face, she didn't let on. "It doesn't matter anyway." Each exhale looked like she was losing something, each inhale like the air was frozen glass.

The winter water beat at the crystal sand. The wind screeched. And somewhere far away, maybe in another world entirely, a crowd of happy people roared and music played. Homer's feet moved him toward a large piece of driftwood. His legs sat him down and his hands reached for a sand-polished stone so they'd have something to hold, so they wouldn't reach for Mia's. "I don't get it. Why couldn't you stay in Florida? D.B.

and Christian care about you. They want to help. We all want to. Why, this one time, couldn't you stay?" Homer looked at the rock as he rolled it between his fingers. It had small flecks of silver sprinkled throughout the gray. "I told D.B. and Christian to hire you. Told my little brother . . . We drove over fifteen hundred miles and you weren't sure what would be at the end? Why not just stay?"

Mia winced. "Because I couldn't."

"I don't understand."

"I don't know." Mia threw her hands up in the air. "Because . . . because for a lot of reasons. Because sometimes seeing how your . . . seeing your family together hurts so much it feels like my heart could stop. Because D.B. and Christian wanted you and Einstein so, so badly and they kept you . . . and didn't give up. And my mom did. She gave me up because . . . And then no one. Else. Wanted. Me." Mia wiped her sleeve across her eyes, took a shaking breath, and continued. "I couldn't stay because the pain was too much and moving on is what I've always done. You can't hate me for not trusting things that seem too good to be true."

"I don't hate you, Mia. I couldn't." Homer had to fight the instinct to stand up and wrap his arms around her.

"I want you to know I wanted to be the person you thought I was. I wanted to be who you saw." Mia was gasping like she couldn't get enough air. Her fingers fumbled with the zipper of her coat. But fabric kept getting caught in the metal. Her fingers kept slipping.

Homer felt his own eyes prick. His heart flooded with wet concrete. "Here." He stood up, tugged a fold of fabric on her coat until the zipper was free. Mia's grateful look was a wave crashing on his concrete heart. In a beat or two, it was his heart again. The one that loved the Anywhere Girl with the fruit-punch hair and the strange sayings and the animal shapes in the clouds. "I'm sorry. Look, can we go somewhere warm? There was that diner by the parking lot. We drove by it, remember? We'll wait for Einstein and Sid. Call the dads. They'll want you to come home."

Mia sniffled. Smiled, catching tears in the corners of her mouth. Wiped her face. "Sure. Okay." She turned, hesitated, found the opening to the path they had taken between the scraggly bushes, and started plodding through the sand. Homer let her get a few feet ahead of him before he followed. Neither one of them said a thing until the water was hidden by the dunes.

Mia stopped so suddenly Homer almost ran into her. "I need to go."

"Okay. We can get a hotel tonight—"

Mia shook her head. "Can I use the Banana? I need to do something—alone."

"Sure. Yeah. The keys." Homer bent his face close enough to his shoulder to wipe his eyes against his shirt collar as he reached into his pants pocket. "How long will you be gone?" Homer glanced at his cell phone. It was hours later than he'd thought. At some point the gray sky had gone mostly black and the crooked streetlights had switched on.

"Just a bit. Not long." Mia looked out straight, but if she saw anything, her eyes gave no hint. She was a sand person, unsteady and as heavy as a broken heart.

"Okay. I'll tell Einstein and Sid to meet us at the diner." There was paper in Homer's throat and the center of him pounded and whirled like he had swallowed the ocean. All of it. Every last drop.

Mia nodded, once at the view, then at Homer. "Thank you." Her feet were too heavy to lift, so she dragged them, leaving two messy lines behind her, a trail to prove she had been there, that it wasn't just Homer's imagination.

Homer sat in the Glory-Be Twenty-Four-Hour Diner for a long time. He texted Einstein, drank coffee, and watched the shapes that the neon signs on the other side of the parking lot made across the large windows.

When he was too jittery to sit still, Homer walked, not realizing until he was standing in front of Trisha's small house that that was where he had intended to go. It was way too late for a stranger to show up, but Trisha answered the door. Insisted Homer come in. *I'm up all night,* she explained. *This one,* she said, gesturing at Goober, *is a pain-in-the-ass night owl. You look a lot like a cousin of mine. That makes you almost-family.* Trisha made coffee, which Homer only sipped to be polite.

No, Mia never came back.

Does she know anyone around here?

I'm sure she just got lost or ran out of gas or something like that.

Maybe it was the way Trisha's sea-glass eyes could hold so much sympathy. Or the steadiness of her gaze, the way she unflinchingly listened like nothing Homer could tell her would shock her. Whatever the reason, Homer found himself rambling about the trip and Mia until the cozy, neat, tiny house began to feel too warm and he needed to walk again. So despite Trisha's invitation to stay, Homer wrote down his phone number and walked back into the night.

He didn't know where else to go, so he went back to the diner. He ordered food he didn't eat because he didn't want to be rude and because the woman behind the counter, Melissa, called him "sweetheart" in a way that seemed like she meant it. He got so many messages from Einstein—*Apollo's playing another encore. This is the best night of my life!!!! See how close we got to the stage?!!!*—that he turned off the sound on his phone.

He was still at the same table—a piece of barely touched something-something pie that Melissa had insisted he try in front of him—when Einstein and Sid burst through the diner door.

"Homes. Uh, where's the car?" Sid said. His nose and cheeks

were red from the cold and his smile was so wide it looked frozen in place. "We cut through the parking lot and the Banana
wasn't in the spot."

"Mia took it," Homer said flatly.

"Like, borrowed it?"

"No, *took it* took it. As in 'took off.' I don't think she's coming
back." Homer sounded as hollow as he felt. *It's not so bad—feeling
empty.* He stood up. Frowned. Einstein was standing behind Sid
like he was trying to hide. "Steiner, what happened?"

Einstein peeked around Sid just enough for Homer to see
that he was holding his left arm to his chest like it was made of
crystal instead of muscle and bone.

"He was feeling the music and—" Sid started to say.

"Is it broken?" Homer interrupted.

"Yeah." Einstein crept forward the same way he tiptoed
around the neighbor's German shepherd.

"Wrist or arm?"

"Just my wrist. I think."

"How?"

"Well, the human wrist is made up of eight different bones
with the scaphoid being the most commonly—"

"I'm not asking for an anatomy lecture, Einstein. I'm asking
how you broke it."

"Right. Uh. I was helping someone."

"A blond-haired female someone," Sid said.

Einstein kicked a piece of crust on the floor next to the counter in Sid's direction. "And I helped her rescue something she dropped at the concert."

"A teddy-bear-that-she-was-trying-to-throw-on-the-stage-from-the-dance-pit something." This time Sid knew to stand out of range of possible pastry missiles.

"Can you guys cool it for one second?"

Einstein and Sid were so quiet Homer wasn't sure they were breathing. "I'm sorry. I'm tired. And the idea of calling the dads to explain how I let my little brother break his wrist at an Apollo Aces concert is not how I wanted to end this shitty, shitty night. What happened exactly?"

"Uh." Einstein coughed. "By the third encore, Sid and I had managed to work our way up to the front. A lovely woman with blond hair got bumped by a group of people jumping up and down, and I fell the wrong way when I tried to catch her stuffed animal before it fell on the ground." Einstein paused, then added, "That thing was so gross and sticky."

"So you broke a bone rescuing a teddy bear at a pop concert."

"Yeah." Einstein shuffled his feet. "What are we going to tell the dads?"

"You better start coming up with a backup story, because I don't think they're going to believe the truth." Homer leaned forward, pressing his clenched fists against his forehead. He shut his eyes and thought out loud. "Okay. We'll ask Melissa to call us a cab. There's got to be a hospital nearby." He opened his eyes and dropped his hands. Both Einstein and Sid were staring at him. "What?"

"Homes, are you okay?" said Sid.

"I'm fine. It's not the end of the world, right? Not until Saturday."

Einstein didn't laugh. In fact, he looked even more worried.

Homer wished he could tell his little brother that it was all going to be okay, that someday this day, the whole trip, would be a funny story, a great remember-the-time-when. But a gear in his chest was stuck. Something inside him had become jammed, and it hurt too much to think, never mind try to lie. "We'll get you some ice. For the ride, okay?"

Einstein nodded.

"Okay." Homer leaned on the counter and waited for Melissa to finish taking an order at the other end. Even with the counter taking some of his weight, Homer felt like gravity was working extra hard to pin him to the earth.

THE HOSPITAL ROOM
OF BROKEN THINGS

EINSTEIN'S WRIST WAS FRACTURED IN two places, the breaks so small the X-ray technician had to take images from four different angles. At least that's what Dr. Arete told D.B. when Homer handed him his phone.

Homer had been hoping Christian would pick up the landline, but he knew the chances were slim. Christian slept like a bear in hibernation. D.B., however, picked up after two rings. So, at a little after four in the morning, Homer had to formulate answers as to how he'd lost the car and Mia and let Einstein get hurt. He had to wait while D.B. gave the head nurse insurance and other info, and then talk to him again, trying to answer questions he didn't have the answers to. When Dr. Arete, the late-night-shift doctor, offered to speak to D.B., Homer gratefully handed off the phone and collapsed into the plastic chair by the bed.

Homer just wanted to sleep. But the doctor kept talking and

talking and winking at Homer like they were coconspirators in something.

"No big deal."

(Wink.)

"All the time. Every day. No problemo. Right. Yup. I have all the information you gave Nurse Halloway right here. Now we just wait for the swelling to go down."

(Wink.)

"Uh-huh. Not a problem. This is the slow time of year. Might as well use the empty rooms. Sure. Yup. Lactose intolerant. I'm sure Halloway got that, but I'll write it down again just to be sure."

(Wink.)

Homer began to wonder if the doctor had something in his eye.

When Dr. Arete covered the bottom of the phone and asked, "Do you want to talk again?" Homer shook his head vigorously and circled his lips in an exaggerated "No" just to be very clear.

Dr. Arete pursed his mouth, nodded, and gave Homer a thumbs-up. "Great. Great. Super. Amazing. We're doing just super here. The cast goes on this afternoon. Right. Need that swelling to go down. We'll keep him comfortable until then. They're quite spectacular young men. Tired? They're exhausted. In fact, it looks like young Homer has nodded off in his chair. . . . Uh-huh . . . yup . . . I'll give him the message myself. Great. Great. Super. Will do. Okay. Bye . . . bye."

Dr. Arete tapped the phone screen with one of his long fingers, then handed the phone to Homer. The plastic case was warm from being pressed against the doctor's face. "Phew. Your father's quite the Chatty Cathy. He says to call after the cast is on."

"Okay. Thank you." Homer slid his phone into his pocket and slumped even lower in his chair. The dry hospital air had been making his eyes sting since he'd been in the waiting area. Or maybe the stinging had started once a nurse had settled the three of them in a little stuffy room that smelled like plastic and disinfectant. *Or maybe*, he thought, *I'm too tired to care.*

Dr. Arete's hand on Homer's shoulder made him jump. "There's an open bed in the doctors' lounge across the hall. Why don't you venture over and get some sleep. Your brother's in great shape and your friend is down for the count." He nodded toward Sid, who was softly snoring in the recliner by the window. The way Sid's long arms and legs hung over the chair's arms made Homer think of Mr. Bentinelli's fried dough draping over the sides of cheap paper plates.

The memory was so close Homer could smell the sun-baked wood of the boardwalk, the greasy sweetness of the dough, the powdered sugar Einstein and he would load on top, the sand, the salt in the air. The need to be home hit Homer's already bruised heart like a baseball bat.

"Sorry, I'm being rude." Homer started to stand, but Dr. Arete stopped him.

"You've had a long night, son." He patted Homer's arm mechanically, once, twice. And then he dropped his hand, hesitating before moving toward the door. "I'll be back in a few hours. But if you need anything in the interim, check in with Nurse Halloway directly. I'll tell her to take good care of you boys."

"Thank you. I will."

"All in a day's work." Dr. Arete had one foot in the hall when Homer stopped him.

"Was there anything else from my dad? Anything other than to call?"

The doctor leaned back so his head was in the room. "He said to tell you he loves you."

"Thank you."

Dr. Arete's pressed-on smile faltered. "You okay, son? If I hadn't seen the X-rays, I'd think you were the one who broke something."

"I'm okay. I'll be okay."

The doctor's white teeth shone once more. The door drifted closed, then clicked shut. The show Sid had been watching on the small TV in the far corner switched to an infomercial for a cordless, stain-detecting vacuum. Homer pushed out of his chair, wincing as the metal legs scraped against the linoleum floor. He glanced at the bed. Einstein's chest rose and fell under the white sheet. In the plastic-covered recliner, Sid snorted, mumbled something, and then went back to whistling softly in and out.

Homer shuffled across the room and shut the TV off just as a guy with inflated muscles said something exciting enough to make a woman in a sweater and tight jeans jump up and down.

Homer opened the closet by the door. There were only two blankets. He spread one over Einstein and tucked the second one around Sid, who smiled but didn't open his eyes.

Homer thought about going to the nurses' station to ask for another blanket and a pillow. But he didn't feel like moving anymore. He sank against the wall opposite the bed, just far enough to the left that he could see Einstein's right hand hanging over the edge.

And for the second night in a row, Homer stared into space, trying to make sense of things that made none.

When he woke up a few hours later, he had a blanket draped over him and Sid and Einstein were arguing about what to watch on TV. For one brief moment, Homer was confused, disoriented by the too-bright fluorescent lights and the way they reflected off the shiny floor.

Then he remembered. He was in a hospital room. He was homesick. And Mia was gone. The hurt began again, so he closed his eyes and hoped that he could will himself back to sleep.

The next time Homer woke up, Sid and Einstein were sitting side by side on the hospital bed. Sid was playing some game with tinny music on his phone while Einstein looked over his shoulder.

At least Steiner got a nerdy friend out of this, Homer thought as he stood up. Maybe it was the word "nerdy," or Einstein's ringtone, but whatever the cause, Homer suddenly remembered the conference. Did Einstein still think they would go to New Hampshire after all this?

"Hi, Dad. Fine. Is D.B. at the airport?" Einstein was miraculously peppy for someone sitting in a hospital bed with two fractured bones.

Homer's knees cracked as he shifted to his feet.

"Buenos días, Señor Homer. Estás bien? Muy bien, gracias. Y tu?" Sid said as he scooted to the end of the bed and picked up the TV remote. He waited just long enough on each channel for the picture to come into focus before he flipped to the next one. "Isn't this amazing? We get all these channels—even the ones with PG-thirteen content. Oh." Sid glanced at Homer. "You don't look so great, Homes. Hey." Sid's face lit up brighter than a marquee. "Have you tried sugar? It's a-*maze*-ing." He held out a sugar packet with the top torn off. "And free. You don't even need to buy coffee."

"You've never had sugar?"

"Nope, not allowed." Sid paused his kicking legs. "Or coffee, come to think of it. Huh." He started swinging again.

"I would hold off on coffee for now." Homer cracked his

knuckles, one hand, then the other. "Since when do you speak Spanish?"

"Excuse me," Einstein interrupted. He tried to cover the bottom of his phone with his left hand, but the thick bandage got in the way. He pressed the phone against his chest instead. "I am on the phone with the dads." He lifted the phone to his ear with a sigh. "As I was saying, the cast will go on as soon as— What? No, navy blue or black. . . . Because orange doesn't go with anything and yellow washes me out." Einstein rolled his eyes and continued chatting.

Sid swung off the bed, stretching his arms above his head as he spoke. "Mercedes is the nurse on duty. She was born in Ecuador. While you were snoring, she taught us 'Good morning' and 'How are you?' and '*Hasta la vista.*'"

Sid's T-shirt had so many stains across the front that it was impossible to tell the original color. Homer stuck his nose in the neck of his own shirt and sniffed. *At least I don't have to worry about Mia smelling me anymore.*

"I'm going to see if the cafeteria has any doughnuts. Mercedes said they're *estupendos*—that's Spanish for 'stupendous.' Want one?" Sid pushed a button on the remote once, twice, a bunch of times, before shrugging and jumping up toward the TV. "Phew. They. Don't. Want." He huffed in between jumps. "This. Off."

Homer crossed in front of Sid. Reached up. Pushed the power button. The screen flashed and then went blank.

"Thanks, Homes." Sid held his fist up for a bump. He looked so goofy and happy to be dirty and smelly and watching TV and eating junk food and hanging out in a place that smelled like lemon cleaner, Homer bumped his fist. He even tried to smile back, but it felt more like a grimace.

Sid stuck both hands on his hips and looked Homer up and down. "Yup. You look like a man who needs a doughnut. Two doughnuts. Doughnuts for everybody." Sid clapped his hands together. He was out the door before Homer could tell him that he wasn't hungry.

"Uh-huh. Uh-huh." Einstein twirled one of the cords attached to the side of his bed around his ankle, then undid it as he nodded. "She might have been doing us a favor. That car was a piece of . . . I wasn't going to say it." Einstein rolled his eyes. "Uh-huh."

Homer shuffled around the bed and sank into the recliner. Someone had opened the blinds on the two windows. *If I squint,* thought Homer, *I can pretend that the strip of blue beyond the parking lot is the ocean. And before that is the beach. And maybe it's getting sucked into the waves so no one else ever has to stand there while someone lets him know he's been a complete idiot.*

"Yup. Yup. I'll tell him. Yup. I love you, too." Einstein started to lift the phone away from his ear, then jerked it back. "You've been feeding Madame Curie, right?" Pause. "It's not disgusting. It's nature. Well, maybe Madame Curie thinks your gluten-free pumpkin muffins are disgusting. Okay. Love you.

Bye." Einstein flung his phone between his feet and flopped back on his pillows. "Would you believe that Christian is squeamish about feeding a starving snake her mice?"

"Huh," Homer said, still staring out the window. Looked down. Looked up. Side to side. Then did it all again.

"So then I said I had been hit by a meteor and dinosaurs were coming back to life while Bigfoot partied with the Loch Ness Monster."

"Uh-huh."

A wrinkled magazine flew to the left of Homer's head, smacked against the window blinds, and fell to the ground. "Oil Tycoon Marries Twenty-Four-Year-Old Starlet." Homer leaned over the recliner's armrest and tilted his head so he could read all the headlines. "Apollo Arrested for Drag Racing in Vegas," he read. "Mother of Nineteen Wants 'Just Five More.'" He sat up. "The articles sound stupid, but your aim has gotten better. Normally you'd miss by feet instead of inches."

"Don't you want to know what Christian told me to tell you?" Einstein moved to cross his arms but remembered that his left was in a splint. Instead he propped his right elbow on the bar meant to keep him from rolling off the bed.

"What's the plan?"

"D.B. couldn't get a flight to Boston today, so he's going to try standby tomorrow. He was going to ask Aunt Anele to come from the city—"

"But she's—"

"In France, I know, so I told him that we would be on our best behavior, get a hotel room, and that he could trust us to take care of ourselves. That he shouldn't rush to get up here."

"Okay."

"Okay? Just okay?"

"Steiner, what else do you want me to say? Whoopee? Hooray? That we get however many more hours of crappy food and shitty television? Sorry if my enthusiasm seems disproportionate to the circumstances." Homer fell back into the recliner and shifted his gaze to the window again. The cars and trees in the parking lot looked like parts of a toy set.

"I was thinking," Einstein said tentatively, "we could still make the conference. Not all of it, but the second day, which is when Dr. Az speaks, so it's the day that matters."

"Steiner." Homer scratched the top of his head, wondering how to say what he needed to say gently. "It's not going to happen. We don't have a car. Remember?"

"Hear me out." Einstein pulled a pad of paper from behind his pillow. "I jotted down some ideas this morning. Number one, we can rent a car, but you'll have to pretend you're twenty-one, which means we need to get a fake ID."

"I'd be the only teenager in the world to get a fake ID to attend a nerd convention." Homer shifted his weight in the recliner, the crack and squeak of the plastic cover making him wish he was home even more.

"It's not a nerd convention." Einstein said "nerd" like it

was a pill he was struggling to swallow. When Homer took his hands away from his face, Einstein's was half hidden by the pad of paper. "Number two, we take the bus. The station's two towns over, so we'd have to get a ride and hope they have taxis where we get dropped off because it's still fifty miles from Grace Mountains."

"D.B. could be here tomorrow if he gets a flight. Sid needs to get home before his parents do. We can't—"

"Number three, we could hitchhike. People might get scared because you're so tall and Sid's been eating a lot of sugar, but I figure that my cast will get us some pity points."

"I can't, Steiner." Homer's eyes ached, and then his words wouldn't come out straight. Everything had fallen apart. "I just . . . I need to go home." He squeezed his hands together until it hurt, but the tears kept coming. He looked up. Einstein's glasses were smudgy and his hair was the craziest it'd ever been. Homer tried to swallow the ball of hurt and disappointment lodged in his throat, but he couldn't, so he whispered instead. "I'm sorry."

"Mia?" Einstein whispered back.

Hearing her name made the ball in Homer's throat slip into his chest. "That and other stuff. What was I thinking? That she'd come back to the island and I'd help her with Tadpole and we'd be this happy little family? Maybe it's that I *wasn't* thinking. Or I thought I was thinking, but wasn't. I am such an idiot." Homer put his face in his hands. They smelled like hospital soap and warm plastic.

Einstein cleared his throat, but Homer couldn't look up. Holding his head felt like it was the only thing keeping his brain from exploding. Einstein talked anyway. "I have a theory I've been working on."

Homer nodded into his hands. "Okay."

"Human beings are like planets. We have individual orbits that overlap in places, but whether or not we meet at the overlaps is all about timing and chance. But that possibility is enough to keep us spinning in circles."

"When the hell did you come up with this?"

"Homer, we've been driving for days. You and Mia were having a lovefest in the front. I was stuck in the back alone, until we picked up Sid. My few choices for entertainment included napping on cracked leather that smelled like rotten fruit and rereading magazines I'd memorized. Staring out the window and pondering the nature of human existence was the best of the options."

Homer whistled. "Touché."

"For what it's worth, she loves you, too."

Homer snorted as he sat up so he could see his little brother's expression. "You think our orbits overlapped."

"Yeah, I do. But I also think her idea of love is a meteor and yours is more like gravity."

"Sounds accurate." Homer wiped his eyes on his arm. "So, what does that mean?"

"Mia doesn't expect good stuff to last and you're the most dependable guy in the world, so—"

"Dependable?"

Einstein shrugged. "You always do the right thing."

Homer rested his elbows on his knees, tilted his head back, and closed his eyes. "Steiner, I think you just graduated from How to Be a Person 101."

"Awesome." Einstein turned on the TV and Homer stared at the ceiling and thought.

UNCLE JOE NO RELATION

IN THE TIME THAT SID was gone, a doctor had switched Einstein from a splint to a cast and Nurse Mercedes had promised she'd have discharge papers to give Homer by the end of her shift.

Homer was going into the bathroom to splash water on his face when Sid came in shouting. "Would you believe someone left a perfectly good package of Yummy! Cakes on a table by the cafeteria?" Sid held his hands above his head and shook two fistfuls of plastic-wrapped sweets. "The ones from the table are strawberry, so I got chocolate and vanilla ones and then I ran out of quarters." Sid stopped in the center of the room and ripped open one of the snacks. A Yummy! Cake with pink frosting fell to the floor. He bent down, brushed it off, and shoved the whole thing in his mouth. "I cawn't beeweave I awte ooof da flur." He swallowed. "Hey, your uncle Joe is out in the hall. He had to take a call, but he said he'd be in in five." Sid bounced as he started to unwrap a second cake. "Is he a businessman? He sounded really important talking on the phone."

Homer and Einstein looked at each other, both confused. "We don't have an uncle Joe," Einstein said slowly. "D.B.'s an only child and Christian's family's all in South Africa, except for Aunt Anele, but she's not married." Einstein turned to Homer. "Aunt Anele didn't get married, did she?"

"No," Homer said as he reached down to pick up a chunk of frosting and sprinkles Sid had missed. "Unless—" Homer saw the guy's sneakers first, followed by jeans, T-shirt, sunglasses, and a zip-up sweatshirt with the hood pulled low on his forehead. Homer stood up. "Uh, hi. Can I help you?"

"This is your uncle Joe." Sid didn't sit on Einstein's bed so much as he jumped onto it.

"Hey," Einstein said, shoving Sid's shoulder with his good arm. "I'm fragile. As a penalty for inflicting bodily injury, I demand a Yummy! Cake."

Sid had a ring of sugar around his mouth and had somehow gotten pink frosting in his hair. "Aye, aye, Captain." He tossed a slightly flattened package at Einstein's chest.

"Hey, if now's a bad time, I can come back." The guy in sunglasses pointed to the door. "I don't want to, ya know, intrude." He shuffled back and forth, glancing at his phone when it vibrated and then shoving it in his jeans pocket.

Einstein paused from trying to press a pillow over Sid's face. "Sorry, do I know you?"

"Nah, not really, man." The guy gave certain vowels a country twang, stretching them like pieces of saltwater taffy. He slid his hood off. His hair was jet-black with streaks of blue and stiff with gel.

Sid gasped. "No way."

The guy pushed his sunglasses on top of his head as he extended his hand to Homer. "I'm—"

"Apollo Aces!" Einstein shouted.

Homer looked at his brother, then at the guy, who was still holding out his hand. He reached out and shook it without thinking. "Oh, shit! I forgot." Homer's hand was sticky with the frosting he'd cleaned off the floor, and now, so was Apollo's.

"Nah, man it's cool. Breaks the ice." Apollo sniffed his hand. "Smells good. Strawberry?"

"They're Yummy! Cakes," Sid shouted. His body was rigid, and his mouth, still coated with sugar, hung open. "I'm your biggest fan."

"Me, too," Einstein didn't shout as loud as Sid, but he looked just as stunned. "Do you want one?" Einstein held the flattened package out as though he was surprised to find it in his hand.

Homer couldn't help it—he laughed. He laughed so hard he had to bend over to breathe. He laughed so hard it was impossible to speak. "You . . . two . . . ri . . . di . . . q . . . lusss." Sid's and Einstein's puzzled expressions only made him laugh harder. When he could finally stand up, he had the hiccups. "Sorry. *Hic.* I'm—*hic.* Sleep—*hic.* De—*hic.* Prived."

Apollo laughed. "No worries. We've all been there." He held up his hands. "I'd slap you on the back or something for the hiccups, but probably should rinse off first."

"The bathroom's—" Sid shouted.

"Behind you." Einstein finished.

"Awesome. One sec."

Homer held his breath for as long as Apollo was rinsing his hands, but he still had the hiccups when Apollo shuffled out of the bathroom, wiped his hands on his jeans, and grabbed a gym bag from the floor in front of the closet.

Even the way he walks is cool, Homer thought as Apollo sat down in the plastic chair and set the bag between his legs. Out loud, the only thing Homer said was *"Hic."*

"Yeah. So." Apollo scratched the back of his neck. "My tour manager told me— Wait. Let me start over." Apollo leaned forward, his elbows on his knees, one hand wrapped around the other. "Your name's Einstein Finn and you got hurt at my concert last night, right?"

"Yes, Mr. Aces." Einstein tried to sit up but couldn't with Sid's weight pinning down the sheets. "But it was just an accident. I—"

"You were helping a woman who was trying to throw a teddy bear onstage during my final encore? My staff filled me in."

"I'm Sid and that's Homer, Einstein's brother, and the encore was awesome." Sid waved his arms so hard that his left elbow cracked against the bed's safety bar. "Ow." Sid clutched his funny bone. "'The Last Song . . . ,'" he said through clenched teeth, "'of . . . Our . . . Lives' . . . is my favorite."

"Cool, man. I worked hard on that one. Glad you like it."

"Love it. Ow."

Homer was grateful the hiccups disguised his laughing.

Apollo unzipped the gym bag and took out a stack of clothing. "Yeah, so the lady you were helping when you got knocked around is, actually, my mom."

"Your mom?" Einstein said, tilting his head just enough to make his glasses slide down his nose.

"Yeah." Apollo replied, ducking his head. "My publicist says it'd be bad for my image if fans knew that my mom comes on all my tours—she's pushing me to do up the whole bad boy, rock star thing." When Apollo looked up his cheeks were flushed.

His ears turn red, too, Homer observed as he leaned against the wall next to the bedside table. *"Hic."*

"So I'm supposed to keep it on the down low and my mom wears a wig if she wants to watch from the front."

"I liked the blond," Einstein said. He still looked a little confused. "And I didn't think she was *that* much older than the other ladies."

Apollo laughed. "I'll tell her you said that. Anyway"—he reached in the bag and pulled out another stack of clothing, T-shirts this time—"you broke your wrist, helping her out, so I had my assistant find out what hospital you ended up in.

Figured the least I could do was say thank you in person and bring some swag." Apollo rummaged through the bag. "I had to get out of the hotel while the most of the paparazzi were distracted." He looked up. "I ordered pizza and had the delivery woman bring it to the vans out front. That part was easy."

"Good . . . *hic* . . . move . . . *hic,*" Homer said.

"Thanks, man." Apollo nodded. "Yeah, so I grabbed a bunch of stuff and just shoved it in here. It's a mishmash: T-shirts, sweatshirts, baseball caps." Apollo tossed items on the bed as he found them. "A signed Frisbee with my face on it?" He held up a purple disk with a picture of him in a tank top in the middle. "Not my idea. Swear."

"Awesome." Sid grabbed the Frisbee. "Can I have this?" He looked at Einstein as he waved the Frisbee.

"Yeah. Of course, you're my best friend, in addition to Homer." Einstein held up a T-shirt with Apollo's profile on the front and "Aces 4 Eva" scrawled across the back. "Homes, this one might fit you."

Homer was still getting over Einstein's calling him his best friend when the T-shirt landed at his feet. "Thanks." He reached down and swept it off the floor. "This is great. And yeah, thank you, Apollo." Homer flung the shirt over his shoulder.

"Don't mention it," Apollo said as he stood up. "Bunch of cheesy concert crap with my face on it is the least I should do." He stretched his arms over his head and yawned. "Though, no offense, looks like you guys could use some clean clothes," he said as he lowered his arms.

"None taken," Sid chimed. He had already pulled a smaller version of the T-shirt Einstein gave Homer over his dirty shirt.

Apollo slid his phone out of his pocket and glanced at the screen. "Seven missed calls. Fifteen new messages. Bet you all of them are from my manager." He shoved the phone back in his jeans. "I should go, but is there a pen around?"

"Here." Homer realized his hiccups were gone as he tossed Apollo the pen from the top of the side table.

Apollo caught the pen with one hand. "Thanks." He picked up a receipt that'd drifted under the bed and wrote. "This is my cell number." He handed the paper to Einstein. "If you need anything or think of something. The tour doesn't leave for Austin until tomorrow afternoon, so just let me know."

Einstein held the scrap in his two hands like he was afraid it would disintegrate. "Thank you. This is so cool."

"So cool," Sid echoed.

"Homer." Apollo shook Homer's hand and clapped him on the back. "Good to meet you. Your little bro's a rad dude. You're lucky."

"Yeah. I know."

Apollo shuffled to the door, paused to slide his sunglasses down and pull on his hood, and then he was gone.

After what felt like a minute of silence, but might have only been seconds, Sid spoke. "If we can watch more TV, this will officially be the best day of my entire life."

"Watch TV and eat Yummy! Cakes," Einstein said as he handed Sid the remote and then ripped open the last package.

Homer's mind had been racing for hours but stopped in an instant. "Yeah." He didn't realize he had spoken out loud until Einstein said "Huh?" But by that time, Homer was already out the door and running.

Homer caught up with Apollo in the parking lot as he was unlocking the door of a huge silver SUV. "Hey, Apollo. One sec."

"Shit." Apollo turned around so quickly his sunglasses clattered to the pavement. "You scared me. Phew. I can see the headlines now." He bent down to pick up the sunglasses. "Badass pop star pisses himself in hospital parking lot." He opened the SUV's driver's-side door and tossed the sunglasses on the passenger seat. "What's up?"

"Sorry." Homer tried to catch his breath as he spoke. "Did . . . you mean it . . . about— Wow, I'm out of shape." Homer took a deep breath. The afternoon air felt amazing after being cooped up in the hospital all morning. "About helping my little brother?"

"Definitely. What's up?"

"Could you help me rent a car?" Homer knew he was rambling but he kept going anyway. "You need to be twenty-one and I'm only eighteen and there's this conference in New Hampshire—it's super geeky—bunch of physicists who research ways the world could be obliterated."

"Go on." Apollo leaned against the car.

"So I'd really like to get him to this conference by tomorrow. The guy who's speaking thinks a black hole— Never
mind, you don't need to know all that. This scientist, Dr. Az,
is Einstein's hero."

"Shit." Apollo stuck his hands in his pockets and kicked the
SUV's rear tire, causing chunks of frozen mud to fall on his
white sneakers. "I'm only twenty, man."

"Oh." Homer felt the adrenaline rush out of him like helium
from a deflating balloon. "Don't worry. I figured it didn't hurt
to ask."

"I can drive you."

"Excuse me?" Homer shaded his eyes so he could see Apollo's face fully.

"I can take you up there tonight. Let the tour bus start driving in the a.m. I'll catch a plane and meet my entourage in
Austin. My tour manager added some buffer days for R and R,
so it's all good."

"You sure?"

"Yeah. I'll just need run back to the hotel, get Sheila—she's
my publicist, super hot, but super scary—to make some phone
calls. I'll grab some of my shit, sneak around the vultures with
cameras, then we can hit the road."

"Einstein should get out in a few hours."

"Cool. Give me two, three tops, to get things in order."

Apollo slapped Homer on the back. "It's cold out here, man. Go inside. Tonight's going to be an adventure."

"Yeah. Okay. Cool. Hey," Homer called just as Apollo shut his door.

Apollo's tinted driver's-side window lowered. "Yeah?"

"I don't mean this in a rude way—but why are you helping us so much? You could have sent a signed T-shirt or something and been done with it."

"Aw, man. Don't get all gushy on me," Apollo said. His head was now completely out the window. "I wasn't always this guy." He pointed at his face in the side mirror. "Once upon a time, I was just a kid, too. Just don't let it slip that I'm not an asshole. Sheila's spent a long time building that image. She'd kill me if word got out."

"Ha." Homer laughed. "Got it." He watched the SUV until it disappeared behind a bend. Apollo was right about the cold and Homer was exhausted, but he wasn't ready to go in. Not yet. So instead of walking toward the sliding doors that led to warmth and sleep, Homer stood in between two rows of cars right where the breeze pulled and pushed the strongest, raised his outstretched arms, and tilted his head to look up at the frozen blue sky.

THE PARABLE OF NOBODY
WHO BECAME SOMEBODY

ONCE THERE WAS A BOY who grew up on the edge of a no-hope town (almost) smack-dab in the middle of America.

This boy had been told by many, many adults (including his own Pop and his chain-smoking Grams) that he wouldn't amount to anything. That he was, and always would be, Nobody.

Nobody was terrible at the things that typically guaranteed a way out of his no-hope town (or, at the very least, a prom date). He was rotten at football, basketball, baseball—anything, really, involving a ball. Academics weren't his strength either. He was hopeless with cars and horrible with computers.

The only time Nobody felt happy and right was on Sunday mornings between eight and ten, when he sang in the choir at the Holy Goodness of Heavenly Light Church.

When Nobody was eight, Ms. Concordia, the young, pretty choir director, gave him his first solo.

When Nobody turned ten, Ms. Concordia married the Reverend and became Mrs. Gould and offered to give him singing lessons before service on Sundays and after Bible study on Wednesdays.

When Nobody was thirteen, Pop left for the final time and Nobody decided that someday he was going to leave his no-hope town, become famous, buy his mom all the nice things she ever wanted, and never feel like Nobody again.

Nobody barely graduated from high school. College wasn't an option—not even the voc-tech would take him after he flubbed his application. But that stuff didn't matter. Not when you wanted out-for-good out, and Nobody was nothing if not patient. Sunday church performances, lessons with Mrs. Gould, and downloaded episodes of *50 States of Talent* made his job at the Dollar + Dime and living with his mom in their too-small trailer bearable.

For over a year, Nobody's life was the same pathetic routine: wake up, go to work, come home, practice, watch TV, go to sleep, and repeat.

But then *50 States of Talent* announced open tryouts in Topeka. Nobody made the three-hour drive on his own. He didn't tell his mom or Mrs. Gould what he was doing. If he failed, Nobody wanted it to be his disappointment alone.

The crazy thing was, he made it to the top ten. Then the top five. Then he was the only one left. Nobody was told to go home and pack some things, because he was flying out to

California to compete against nine other contestants on live TV.

The lady dressed in all black said ITC Entertainment would only pay for two plane tickets. Mrs. Gould said she understood. Nobody needed to take his mom. Mrs. Gould promised that the entire congregation of the Holy Goodness of Heavenly Light would send prayers for his safety and success as high as the sky could carry them.

Those prayers must have gone right up to the celestial penthouse, because, week after week, Nobody kept beating the other competitors, kept moving on to the next round.

"Your @#$%^ range is @#$% amazing! Where the #$%^ have you been #$%^& hiding?" said the music producer, who, as the "Mean Judge," was far better known for his epic on-camera tantrums and sarcasm than he was for saying anything positive—ever.

"Young man, bless. I know your mama's here, but I just have to say that you're hotter than a tin roof in the Texas sun," said the "Nice Judge," whose country-singing career was enjoying an upswing due to her low-cut dresses and her high-profile divorce.

"Pleased to be doing business with you," said the ITC Entertainment CEO, Just Call Me Jim, when he shook Nobody's hand the night he was named "America's Best Talent."

"You'll have to move to Nashville."

"The sooner the better."

"Your mom can come with you, of course."

"She's a real light packer."

"We'll set you up with an apartment. New clothes. A roomful of guitars. Whatever you need."

"Sounds great."

"You're going to have stadiums of fans screaming your name. I'll make sure you have own cologne, action figure, and men's casual clothing line. You won't be able to sneeze without the paparazzi getting a picture of the snot shooting out your nose. Beautiful, talented women will want to date you and the whole #$%^ world will want to be you."

"Don't threaten me with a good time."

Just Call Me Jim made good on his promises—and then some.

Somewhere in between moving from the (almost) middle of America to the center of the country's music metropolis and his first album going platinum, Nobody stopped being Nobody.

He'd become Somebody instead.

THE CAR RIDE OF TRUTH AND
THE MORNING OF THE DAY
THE WORLD COULD END

APOLLO ACES, INTERNATIONAL POP star and the media's favorite crooning bad boy, was a man of his word. When Homer looked outside Einstein's window two and a half hours later, Apollo was leaning against the giant SUV, a baseball cap hiding his face. He was typing on his phone.

"He's here." Homer looked at Einstein and Sid. They'd been sitting side by side on the bed since the nurse had given Homer Einstein's discharge papers. Both of them were dressed head to toe in Apollo Aces apparel. Homer looked down at his own outfit. He'd decided his jeans didn't reek too badly, but he knew the combination of Apollo Aces socks, boxers, T-shirt, and sweatshirt was still over the top.

"What now?" Einstein asked as he swung his legs impatiently.

Homer glanced at his phone. "Now we go to Grace Mountains."

★ ★ ★

"So," Apollo said after they'd turned out of the hospital drive. "Where you guys from?"

"Florida," Einstein said. He kept sliding back on the over-stuffed backseat, no matter how much he tried to scramble forward. "Sid's from Delaware. He's homeschooled."

Apollo laughed. "I'm sorry, man. I hated high school, but still, home school sounds kinda boring."

Sid looked up from examining the countless buttons on the back of the center console. "It is."

"You drove all the way up from Florida for a conference?"

"Not exactly," Einstein replied. Homer glanced back at his brother. He looked like a satisfied king sitting on a throne. "We really drove up for a girl. The conference was my condition for accompanying Homes."

"A girl?" Apollo swiped the baseball cap off his head and tossed it on the dashboard. "She must be something."

Sid's face appeared between the front seats. "Her name's Mia."

"Sid, man. Put your seat belt back on," Homer said, watching Sid until he saw him click his seat belt.

"Fine, but as soon as we hit New Hampshire, I am not legally bound to wear a seat belt."

"Sure." Apollo glanced in the rearview mirror. "But if you don't want to walk, I suggest you keep it on." He turned his eyes back to the road. "So, where's Mia now?"

Homer scratched his head. "It's a long story."

"And we've got over four hours of drive time, so start at the beginning."

Homer leaned forward. Dropped his head to his chest. Inhaled. Exhaled. And began talking. "After the first time I met her, before I knew her name, in my head I called her the Anywhere Girl. . . ."

And for the second time in fewer than twenty-four hours, Homer found himself spilling his story to an understanding stranger.

It would have been easy to miss Grace Mountains completely. The last two hours of the drive were all twisting two-lane roads dotted with potholes that felt large enough and deep enough to swallow a whole car—never mind one or two tires.

By the time Apollo crept by a green road sign that read "Grace Mountains: Two Miles," it was impossible to see anything that wasn't directly lit by the SUV's headlights. Between Sid's snack stops and Einstein's bathroom breaks and traffic once they got on the Kancamagus Highway, the trip had taken twice as long as it should have.

The clouds covered the moon like a piece of clothing carelessly thrown over a lamp, causing buildings to look like boulders and street signs to be unreadable. The glaring whiteness of the snow on the ground made the black of the night that much darker. And every hotel, motel, bed-and-breakfast, or inn they passed had a "No Vacancy" sign up.

"Einstein," Homer said with a yawn. "How many people come to this conference?"

"Lots," Einstein replied, his voice heavy with sleepiness. "Lots and lots."

They had to drive two towns away to find a motel with free rooms.

"Sorry," Homer said once he and Apollo had collected their keys from the apathetic woman at the front desk. "This is probably not what you're used to."

"Nah, don't be." Apollo tossed his key up and caught it. "Fancy places all blur together. This one's"—Apollo looked at the flickering neon "Open" sign over the entrance for registration—"memorable. Reminds me of the place I grew up. Actually, this whole drive, I've been thinking about how long it's been since I've been in that town." He laughed. "Crazy, right? I spent most of my life figuring a way out and now I feel like I owe it to myself to go back."

"Believe me," Homer said, his footsteps falling into the same rhythm as Apollo's as they crossed the frosted parking lot to the SUV where Sid and Einstein were asleep in the backseat, "there are wackier reasons people end up where they do."

On December twentieth, Homer, Einstein, and Sid discovered firsthand how difficult it could be to wake up a pop star who was used to sleeping past noon. The sun was already high in the sky before they got back to Grace Mountains.

"This place is a circus, man," Apollo said as they crept along Main Street that afternoon. "Reminds me of the scene before one of my concerts."

"There's a woman in a tutu and . . . alien ears?" Sid pressed a finger against the SUV window. "Three people dressed as robots. Everyone else looks like Einstein in ten years." Sid slumped down in his seat.

"Ha. Ha. Very funny." Einstein didn't look up from his phone. "Okay, Apollo. You want to take this right turn once all the people are out of the way."

"Aye, aye." Apollo saluted and then gunned the SUV through the first break in the stream of conference attendees.

The road Einstein directed them down became dirt just a few yards after the turn. After the second bend, it led to a weathered barn that guarded a sprawling farmhouse twenty or so feet behind it.

Einstein saw her first. Then Sid. And, finally, Homer turned his head to see what they were gasping about.

And there she was.

This time, there was no pausing.

This time, the universe spun like it hung at the end of a twisted rope.

"Ah, Apollo, you can drop us off here. This is it." Homer pointed to a wooden sign, half hidden by the branches of a winter-naked bush: "Welcome to I-9 Institute for the Study of Probable Doom, Existential Risks, and Apocalyptic Possibilities."

The barn couldn't have been higher than three stories, but its shadow seemed to stretch all the way from the building's sunken base to the beginning of a dirt parking lot where Mia stood, her arms crossed and her fruit-punch hair made even brighter by the bareness of the trees behind her.

Apollo shifted the car into park. "Is that her?" He pointed outside Homer's window.

"Yup." Homer undid his seat belt and hopped out of the car. Sid and Einstein were already standing side by side looking at their feet in the dirt. Homer turned to say good-bye to Apollo, but the driver's seat was empty.

"Hug it out, man." Apollo strode around the front of the car, flipped his cap backward, and pulled Homer into a hug. "Stay good. All right? World needs good guys."

"Yeah," Homer said, stunned. "You, too."

Apollo hugged Einstein. "Stay real, genius. Keep saving other guys' moms."

Then Sid. "Hey, man, you keep crazy. Okay? Gotta let that enthusiasm flow. It's a beautiful thing."

Finally, he turned and crossed the dirt to where Mia was leaning against the Banana's trunk. He shook Mia's hand and said something to her, but the only words Homer could make out were "Be kind."

As Apollo jogged back to the SUV, he shouted, "It's been real, but I gotta split. You have my number. That means you keep in touch. You guys ever want concert tickets . . . whatever.

You got it." Then he hopped in the car, honked the horn, and disappeared down the dirt drive.

"Was that who I think it was?" Mia asked softly as she walked toward them.

"Long story," Einstein said.

"Awesome story," Sid added.

"Sid and I are going to look around," Einstein said, pointing toward the barn.

"We are?"

"Yup." Einstein punched Homer lightly on the arm with one hand and clapped Sid on the back with the other. Then he and Sid crunched over the frozen grass and Homer was alone with Mia.

"I brought back the Banana."

"I see."

Mia shuffled her feet and wrapped her arms around her chest. Looked up. Looked down. "I came back for you. The grumpy guy at the parking lot said he didn't know anything. The lady at the diner said she hadn't worked the night shift. Then I went back to Trisha's just in case you'd gone there, and to the beach. But—"

"How'd you know to come here?"

"Einstein's been talking about this conference for months."

"Oh."

"Homer, I—" Mia swept her foot back and forth across the ground.

"It's fine, Mia." Homer saw Einstein and Sid appear around the corner. "I think I get it now."

Then the side door to the barn at the end of a brick walkway opened and a man in a white lab coat stuck his head out. "You kids know we aren't doing tours today, right? You should have seen that in the conference packet." His voice was high, almost to the point of being squeaky.

"But we drove all the way from Florida," Einstein said, stopping next to Sid a few feet from the door. "And I have a broken wrist."

The man looked Einstein up and down, then sighed. "Oh, come on in. I'll see if we can make an exception. No use freezing your molecules off out here."

"Ha. Get it? Molecules off." Sid was the first one through the door, followed closely by Einstein. Homer didn't turn around to see if Mia was coming, but he heard one more set of footsteps follow him in.

MEETING THE WIZARD
WHO WAS JUST A MAN

WHEN THE DOOR SWUNG SHUT, they were left in total darkness. The air smelled like sawdust and stale coffee and the floor was cold stone with a layer of grit that scratched and scuttled under the many pairs of shifting feet.

"Hello?" Sid's whisper echoed like they were in a cave instead of a barn.

"What brings you to this place?" The robotic voice was loud enough to make dust sprinkle from above.

No one answered. The only sounds were those of grit grinding beneath shoes and dust pinging against the floor.

"I said, what brings you to this place?" This time there was a short chime that sounded like a computer being turned on, and then a giant green face appeared on the wall behind them as smoke crept around their feet like a herd of friendly cats. The air smelled like chemicals, something dry and vinegary, and the giant face, which looked like a Halloween mask altered and angled to appear futuristic—the eyes were just slits, the cheekbones triangles—hovered a few feet in the air. Homer had to think deliberately about unclenching his hands before his fingers obeyed, and when he looked at the others, their faces tinted green by the light coming off that face, he saw reflections of his own confusion. Mia was biting her lip. Sid looked stunned. Einstein's face was a mixture of awe and terror. The guy in the lab coat had disappeared. And suddenly, Homer was angry. Really, really, really angry.

"What brings—"

"Look," Homer yelled. "We've driven more miles than I want to count. We've been bossed around by strangers, lost, bored, hungry, freezing, boiling, and . . . sad." Homer took a breath and kept going. "We've survived crazy people, mean people, and leaving places we wanted to stay, so if you could just cut the bullshit, I would appreciate it."

"Oh." The huge mouth in the huge face formed a circle, and then the face disappeared. A moment later, the barn was flooded with light.

"Awesome!" Einstein shouted, and when Homer could fully open his eyes, he had to agree.

The inside of the barn could just as well have been the interior of a spacecraft. Except for the door leading to a dark hall, the space was open. To their immediate right was a shiny, sterile-looking area with things made of stainless steel, glass beakers, test tubes, and other lab apparatus dotting its countertops. A large modern table surrounded by clear plastic chairs was set up in the far corner, and the rest of the floor was taken up by desks overflowing with books, papers, and a bunch of other stuff.

"My apologies. I didn't mean to frighten you." A short man with deep-brown skin and a gray beard streaked with black and dark orange appeared in the doorway, his arms firmly behind him. "Usually, visitors are amused. We start every tour this way. A hologram expert from M.I.T. once praised its intricacies. As far as green faces go, it seems this one is distinctive." He sighed. "But I digress. Welcome to I-9."

His voice, Homer noticed, had a particular cadence to it, a rhythm that made each sentence sound like he was reading poetry.

"I'm Dr. Az. Please come in." He gestured toward the area in the corner closest to the doorway and next to the lab. "Take a seat."

The four of them moved like stunned zombies to the various stools and chairs Dr. Az had indicated.

"I have a question," Sid said. He was perched on the edge of the chair next to Einstein's. "What's with the hologram?"

"Why do I use it?" Dr. Az smiled. "Part of the reason is laziness, pure and simple. Dr. Fischer put it up three years ago as a practical joke, and week after week we neglect to take it down. It's a bit like brown Christmas wreaths in spring or a lawn ornament half buried in snow." Dr. Az sighed. "But mostly, I keep it up for the visitors. More leave upset than elated, and I believe the hologram gives even the most disappointed ones a story to tell."

"Why are so many upset?" Mia asked softly, looking up from her lap.

"Because they arrive expecting a wizard, and I am just a man. They want a cathedral to the future and find an old barn instead. They come hoping for answers and only leave with more questions."

"But why would they leave with more? Einstein says you're the smartest guy in the world." Mia's voice was stronger now.

"Because they say they're here to learn the fate of the world, how it will end and when. But I can't give them an answer—not for those questions, not for the many others that also brought them here."

"Why—" Einstein started to say.

"That's how many of the questions start: 'Why.' What a terrible, wonderful word."

Dr. Az stepped to a dented globe, walked his fingers from Canada to Australia, and then around and around again. "We could have remained a bunch of atoms darting about in the darkness like cosmic bumper cars. But we didn't. You'd think 'Why are we here at all?' would be the most popular question. But in my nearly thirty years with I-9, I have heard so many more."

He stuck his hands behind his back again and started pacing. "Why are there hangovers, death, frizzy hair, and speeding tickets? Why do pets die and best friends move away? Why does milk spoil and why do species go extinct? Why do people use faith to justify terrible things and why is righteousness so often offered as a reason instead of what's right?"

When Dr. Az's back was to them. Homer tried to catch Einstein's eye, but his brother's gaze was pinned to Dr. Az, who was now weaving through the large room, picking things up, inspecting them, then setting them down.

"Why are some souls crushed and some dreams never fulfilled? Why are some people born poor and some people born rich? Why are movie tickets so expensive and why is food that's bad for you so cheap? Why are animals neglected and children allowed to go hungry? Why do ballerinas fall and planes crash? Why do parents get old and grandparents get sick?"

Dr. Az stopped in front of a sculpture of a woman in a lab coat and started polishing the plaque on the base with his sleeve. "Who knows? I don't. Dr. Greenfield"—he pointed at the statue—"doesn't, I mean didn't." He stared past the statue as though he had already forgotten it was there. "And she was the greatest biologist the world has ever seen."

"I'm sorry," Mia whispered. "For your loss."

Dr. Az looked puzzled. "Thank you. That's kind of you to say."

He kept pacing, but slower now. "Perhaps it's because we are the products of broken-down stars or it's that the world actually spins counterclockwise from the south and Pluto is a planet after all." He picked up a tennis ball that was more brown than yellow and tossed it back and forth between his hands.

"Perhaps. Perhaps. Perhaps. Perhaps, more often then not, suffering has no meaning and cannot be anticipated. Perhaps the future, the present, and the past are all full of unknowable unknowns. Perhaps this is not a problem we can solve." Dr. Az sighed and set the tennis ball in a coffee mug. "It's a paradox we need to accept."

Dr. Az used one of the stools to lift himself onto the lab table. He sat down, crossed his arms, and swung his legs. "Forgive me. I've always found this time of year to be melancholic. In a December, more years ago than I like to count, I left the country where I was born for a new life. I wasn't much older than you." Dr. Az nodded at Homer, then at Mia. "And here I haven't told you anything about the Institute or let you ask any questions." He shifted to face Sid. "Why don't *you* start? What brings you here today?"

"Oh, I didn't want to come here, I just wanted to get out of Delaware. Shoot." Sid's face went from interested to stricken. "It's not that this isn't awesome, but, it's just, I was only along for the ride."

Dr. Az smiled. "I'm not offended. Go on."

"Uh, I don't have anything else. It's been great. I made friends. Home is going to seem incredibly boring after this. I probably won't do anything cool again until I turn eighty."

"What's your name, young man?"

"Sid. It's short for Siddhartha."

"Are you familiar with the Law of the Conservation of Matter?"

"Yes, sir. I'm advanced for my age."

"Then you know that when matter changes from one form to another in a closed system—a vacuum, so to speak—that matter stays constant. Nothing lost. Nothing gained. However . . ." Dr. Az paused. "Life is far from a closed system, and thus a changed life cannot stay constant. It's forever altered. Understand?"

Sid's eyebrows were furrowed, but he nodded.

Dr. Az looked at Einstein expectantly.

"Hi. I'm Einstein."

Dr. Az drummed his fingers on the metal table. "Good name."

"Thanks. My brother chose it." Einstein pointed at Homer.

"Good brother," Dr. Az quipped.

"Thanks," Homer said, staring down at his hands.

"I just need to say that I have wanted to visit I-9 since I decided to write my dissertation on existential risks," Einstein said. "And it's more amazing than I could have dreamed and . . . and so awesome to meet you."

"You drove—how did you put it?" Dr. Az glanced at Homer. "I think it was 'more miles than can be counted.' You did this just to see an old man, an ancient prophet of doom and gloom?"

"You're the greatest physicist since, well, Einstein." Einstein flung his arms out to his sides, forgetting that he had a cast on his left wrist and that Sid was sitting next to him.

"Ow."

"Sorry, Sid."

"No worries," Sid said, rubbing his shoulder.

"I see," Dr. Az said, his voice steady and his gaze unnervingly even. "As flattered as I am, evidence suggests that meeting me is hardly the highlight of your undertaking."

Einstein looked like he was thinking of protesting but then shrugged.

"Young lady." Dr. Az crossed his arms again when he turned to Mia. "What brings you to the second annual I-9 Institute for the Study of Probable Doom, Existential Risks, and Apocalyptic Possibilities Conference on the Significant Dangers and Slim Rewards of the Giant Atom Accelerator?"

"Oh, I'm not supposed to be here," Mia said apologetically. "I drove up to say 'sorry' to Homer." She pointed across the table at him. "Not for the conference. But," she added, "your barn is very nice. I'm glad I got to see it. Very old meets new."

Dr. Az clapped his hands. "This may be the easiest group I'll ever have." He shifted, indicating that Homer's turn was next. "Though there's always room for a grand inquiry about the cosmos."

"I think . . ." Homer looked up from the floor, letting his eyes meet Dr. Az's. "I think that I'm still coming up with questions."

"But you'll get there?" Dr. Az said.

Homer half smiled. "Yeah. I think I will."

"Good." Dr. Az hopped off the lab table. "Now you young people will have to excuse me. I have a keynote speech to finalize and I believe you're already late for the party." Dr. Az squinted at his watch. "Yes, six twenty-two. It's begun."

"Party?" Sid asked as he shook Dr. Az's hand.

"It'd be rude to meet the end of the world without one." Dr Az replied. He clapped his hands twice and a light turned on over the now-open door. "Even ruder to not celebrate humanity's survival if that's the direction the night takes."

Einstein followed Sid, then Mia followed, and finally Homer shook Dr. Az's hand and moved toward the door.

"Homer?"

Dr. Az's voice made Homer pause a few feet from the exit and the new night. "Yes, sir?"

"We're all just bunches of atoms, the same ones that were here at the beginning."

Homer swallowed. "Right. I know. The Big Bang."

"The atoms that make up you, the ones that make up me, they just as easily could have formed the rings of Jupiter, a comet, or one of the innumerable stars."

"Oh, that's neat." Homer wasn't sure how he was supposed to respond, and the awkward way he had turned was starting to make him wobble.

"A great poet led me to this understanding. Not Galileo,

Mitchell, or even your brother's namesake." Dr. Az pressed two fingers to his temple as if he needed the pressure to remember. "The stars are watching, and they envy us," Dr. Az said, lowering his hand. "Our atoms got lucky, Homer, yours and mine. They got to become human. To waste a moment of that cosmic blessing would be an insult to the not as fortunate stars."

"I think I understand."

Dr. Az nodded. "Good."

THE PARABLE OF THE
FUTURE MAD PHYSICIST

IT TOOK YEARS FOR THE Future Mad Physicist to
get used to the wet cold of North America. It was so very different from the cold of the country where he was born, which
was a dry desert cold that even at its January worst stayed above
freezing. Perhaps the contrast wouldn't have seemed so drastic
if the years that the Future Mad Physicist spent in the refugee
camps hadn't been so hot.

The day of his final resettlement interview had been particularly brutal. The Future Mad Physicist had nearly fainted as he sat
on a metal chair trying not to choke on the plastic-baked air in
one of the imposing white tents just outside the camps. It could
have been the heat or it could have been the fear: he was terrified
of answering the uniformed man's questions incorrectly. If he did
well, he would join his father's brother in America. If he failed,
he would have to stay. A life in the camps. A life spent in neither

Here nor There, but somewhere In Between.

The Future Mad Physicist had always been a diligent student. He studied the interview questions for months, preparing two answers (one spoken, one silent) for each.

Do you believe you were persecuted for your religious beliefs in your country of origin?

Spoken: *Yes.*

Silent: *Persecuted? It seems such a trivial word when death is the price so many have paid for having a faith that those in power don't share.*

Should you return to your country of origin, do you think your life would be in danger?

Spoken: *Undoubtedly.*

Silent: *The men who came for my father were neighbors—men he trusted. He went with them, thinking he was walking in the direction of negotiation and peace. I hope the moment that he realized he was moving toward his grave was only seconds before they killed him. These men know my face. Returning home would be a death sentence.*

Do you find it difficult to procure necessities, such as food, water, and clothing, in the refugee camps?

Spoken: *Life in the camps isn't easy, sir. But I am grateful to be here. Many have not been as fortunate.*

Silent: *I wish I were a poet. Then I could spin words in such a way that you would understand what it's like to run from one hell into another, more terrible and soul-crushing than the one before. In the camps, I have come to understand that hunger can hurt in your bones and that not being able to do anything, not even cry, to ease another's suffering is the cruelest torture on Earth.*

I am only a young man, but in my twenty years of life, I have witnessed such pain and loss that my father's faith has been taken from me. I am no longer afraid of death. But I have much to do before it arrives.

If granted asylum in the United States, what will you do to become a contributing member of society?

Spoken: *I plan on enrolling in an American university as soon as possible after my arrival. I will become a scientist.*

Silent: *I'll make it my life's work to find explanations where most think there are none. I'll try to do good and avoid doing harm. I'll become a man my father would have been proud to call his son.*

The Future Mad Physicist was older than most of the other first-years at the American university where Amu, his uncle, taught literature and poetry. He seldom had a class outside the science building and never took one of Amu's courses, but on the day his uncle was teaching Rumi, the Future Mad Physicist snuck into the literature auditorium to listen to his uncle read.

"A moment of happiness . . ."

The Future Mad Physicist closed his eyes and let the words wrap around him.

"We feel the flowing of life here, you and I. . . ."

For the span of the class, he let himself imagine that the voice reading his father's favorite poet was indeed his father and that the smells of the classroom (air freshener and new paper) were replaced by those of the city where he once lived (rose water and fine dust).

"The stars will be watching us,

. . .

In one form upon this Earth,
and in another form in a timeless sweet land."

The Future Mad Physicist was so deep in his memories that he didn't realize that the class was over until he felt Amu's hand on his shoulder.

"Rahman Joon," Amu said. "Are you well?"

"Yes," he answered, even though he wasn't.

He would be.

Someday.

The future, he reasoned, was as good a thing as any to believe in.

THE WATCHING OF
THE END OF THE WORLD

"WHAT DO WE DO NOW?" Sid asked once the huge door had shut behind them. "It's cold out."

"We go to the party and wait for the end of the world," Homer said softly as he started walking toward the farmhouse, where every window was a glowing rectangle and a jazzy song in a language he couldn't place pushed out from under the front door, skittering across the porch like each note was a crystal tossed by an invisible hand.

Einstein lightly punched Homer's arm as he jogged up to his left, Sid beside him. Mia stepped silently to Homer's right side. As a straight line of four, they crunched over the frozen grass, moving from the dark to the light.

The farmhouse's entry room narrowed to a hallway before opening into a ballroom-like space packed with conference goers. In the far corner, a few couples waltzed to the strange music while circles of men in wrinkled suits and women in dresses that sparkled spoke in shoulder-to-shoulder groups throughout the room. Sid and Einstein made a beeline for the food tables just a few steps into the party, leaving Homer and Mia alone.

Homer pointed to the set of bleachers just to the right of the dance floor. "Want to sit down?"

Mia shrugged. "Okay."

Homer took longer than he needed to figure out how to fit his legs behind the second row of seats. When he finally stopped squirming, Mia didn't say anything. For half a heart-beat, he wasn't sure she would.

"Trisha said you came back, to look for me." Mia kept her eyes on her hands as she spoke.

Homer swallowed. "Yeah. I thought maybe you'd go there." He couldn't tell if he was turning red or if the top row of bleachers was the stuffiest place in the room.

"She likes you." Mia smiled sadly. "She said you were one of the good ones."

"She's really nice. I think her life hasn't been easy—either," Homer added lamely.

Mia glanced sideways at him. "Maybe that's why she said I could have the apartment."

"What?" The two women in the second row glared over their shoulders at Homer.

"Shhhh," the taller of the two whispered. "Dr. Az is going to speak."

Homer glanced at the front of the room. The groups of

talkers had been pushed back to create a half circle of open space. The only thing there so far was a lonely microphone on a stand. "Did you say yes?"

"I—"

Sid and Einstein clambered up the bleachers, each balancing an overloaded plate, and sat down in the row in front of Homer and Mia before Mia could finish answering.

"They have brownies," Sid said, smiling so widely it seemed like he was using his chocolate-covered teeth as proof.

"Quiet. Az is speaking." Einstein nudged Sid and pointed to the microphone, where Dr. Az now stood.

Thank you. This might be our largest conference yet.

Dr. Az's voice was deep and smooth. If he had been nervous about speaking, it didn't show.

Thank you to my colleagues at I-9 who graciously donated valuable research time to conduct workshops and deliver papers. What an opportunity, to hear from the world's greatest thinkers addressing the world's greatest problems. Thank you to participants who have come from all over to be here tonight. I'd like, in particular, to recognize our youngest participants, who drove a great distance in search of knowledge.

Sid punched Einstein's shoulder "That's us!"

"Ow."

Now, we only have one hour and fifteen minutes before the end of the world. So I'd better get started.

Some people chuckled. Many, including the women who

had given Homer nasty looks, did not.

Dr. Az waited for the crowd to settle before he pressed on. When he did, Homer whispered to Mia, "Are you going to?"

She nodded. "I'll take care of Baby Goober to pay rent. Tadpole will have someone to play with. There's already furniture and stuff. . . ." Mia's voice trailed off.

>*The world will cease to exist one day. That is certain. But how and when—that's the mystery. The universe began with a bang—but it could end with a whisper.*

Homer heard Dr. Az, but not really. It was like his words drifted into Homer's ears but couldn't reach his spinning brain.

"Do you—" Mia stopped speaking when the tall woman gave her a look that could have melted ice.

Homer gestured toward the door that someone had propped open near the end of the bleachers. Mia made an "okay" sign with her hand and carefully slid in that direction. Homer touched Einstein's shoulder to let him know where they'd be.

His little brother's glasses were smudged, he had crumbs on his shirt, and when Einstein mouthed "Good luck," Homer wished he had space to hug him. He settled for pretending to mess with his hair and silently replying, "Thank you." Then he followed Mia into the night.

>*Mankind is so arrogant and foolish as to believe that the story of the universe could be any different from the stories we tell. The stories that all have a beginning. A middle. An end.*

Dr. Az's voice followed them to a picnic table at the base of a small snow-covered hill. Homer watched Mia pick a spot before he hopped up and sat beside her on the top of the table.

Homer waited for a round of applause to die down before he spoke. "Why? Why Glory-Be if Dotts isn't there?"

Mia looked at her hands. "It's more a feeling than a reason—something telling me that it's where I need to be, for now at least. I know that sounds silly." She picked at imaginary strings on her coat. "I can take classes at the community college. Trisha said that I could borrow her car and that she'd teach me how to cut hair. I think I'd like it, cutting hair, making people happy."

Homer tilted his head back and fixed his eyes on the stars. *If you believe in gravity, you already believe in something higher than yourself.* Out loud he said, "I think you are so much smarter than you give yourself credit for."

Even people of science must have faith.

"You mean that?" Mia crunched the heel of her sneaker on a patch of ice that clung to the picnic table's bench.

"Of course I do."

Mia smiled shyly as she gathered the broken ice into a pile with her foot. "Did you know Tadpole's dad wanted to marry me? He proposed over the phone when I told him I was pregnant. Said he still didn't know why I left, yada yada yada." On the final "yada," Mia kicked the pile of broken ice she'd created into the air.

The bits that made it far enough to catch the light from the open door glistened like pieces of a broken chandelier before disappearing into the snow.

So we keep tying our shoelaces.

"Why'd you say no?" Homer tempered the jealousy that sparked in his chest.

And turning car keys.

"Because I need to prove something to myself. I don't know what, but it's important."

Doing dishes, mowing lawns, and brushing our teeth.

"You'll find out what."

We keep praying and asking and breathing and loving—

"You will, too."

Because it's an imperfect miracle of atoms and chaos that we are here at all.

"Plus, I was already in love with you." Mia's voice shook as she spoke. "And before you say anything, I want you to know that I know I've got things to figure out and that stealing the Banana was so, so wrong."

"If you had let that car roll off the side of a mountain, you would have been doing the dads a favor." Homer's heart felt like it was pressing against his lungs. *Mia said she loved me? She. Loves. Me. Back.*

"It really is hideous." Mia sniffled. "Isn't it?"

"And it smells. We could leave the keys in the ignition and put a sign that says 'Steal Me!' on the windshield and no one would touch it."

Mia's laugh cut through the cold air like lightning slicing

through clouds. "You're special, Homer. You don't see it yet, but I hope you do soon." Mia tilted her head to the side. "Can I kiss you?"

Our species is so young and so ancient.

"Not because you feel bad for me?"

Mia shook her head. Tears, clear pebbles of salt water, had drifted down her cheeks.

"Then why?"

"Because I want to."

We are so tough with our souls of brick and iron.

"Okay."

We are so fragile with our hearts of paper and glass.

Mia's lips were chilly and soft when she pressed them to Homer's neck, but warm by the time she'd kissed her way to his mouth. In the pause between, when Mia's lips hovered just above his, Homer gently wrapped his hand around the back of her neck, bringing her as close as he could, carving a pocket out of the night that began and ended with them. Her skin felt smooth even to his cold fingertips. He could count her heart beating through a vein in her neck. *One. Two. Three.*

Then they kissed and the universe came rushing in and the pocket they'd created exploded and Homer realized that that was okay and he let himself fall into the uncertainty because he understood now the unpredictability of it all.

The kiss was wonderful and amazing, but also sad. Most good-byes are.

Maybe a thousand years from now we will no longer recognize ourselves as we are today.

When Mia pulled away, Homer watched the white clouds of her breath blend with his, drifting upward, until they disappeared and became part of the cloudless night.

And maybe in a thousand years we will still be trying to understand just how to be.

Mia wrapped her hand around the back of Homer's neck and he kept his on hers. He needed to be touching her to be strong enough to say what he needed to say.

Maybe we will have the same questions and the same lack of answers.

"That was a good-bye, wasn't it?" Homer said, touching his forehead to hers.

It doesn't matter.

"Not a forever one," Mia whispered. "It's a let's-see-what-happens good-bye. Besides"—she laughed even as tears slid from her eyes to her chin—"I need one last ride. To Glory-Be."

Homer smiled and used the sleeve of his coat to wipe off her cheeks. "Well, you'll get to see a very angry D.B. Tomorrow morning's the first flight he could get. Einstein and I are supposed to meet him in Boston. At least now we can drive."

We—

"Can I have the cameras?" Mia pressed her face into Homer's neck. The warmth and realness of her made it hard for him to swallow.

Will—

"Sure. You'll have to find a place that develops film."

Still be—

"I'll send you copies. But only of the good ones. There are probably a million bazillion photos of the floor mats and Einstein and Sid snoring in the backseat."

Here.

"Promise."

"It might take me a while."

"I've heard that stuff that matters takes time."

Mia leaned her head against Homer's chest. For a moment, they watched white shards shower down from snow-heavy branches and fall through the dark sky to join the luminous covering on the ground.

And this flawed, exquisite existence—

"Should we go back in?" Mia whispered.

It—

"Nah. This is probably the best place on the planet to wait."

Is—

"For the world to end?"

Reason—

"Or not. You never know."

Enough.

There was nothing else Homer could say, so he rested his head on top of Mia's and wrapped his arms around her for as long as the universe would give him.

THE PARABLE OF
THE END OF THE WORLD

ONCE UPON A TIME, in a solar system in a galaxy known as the Milky Way on a planet called Earth, a boy and a girl sat side by side on a picnic table at the bottom of a snow-covered hill, holding each other as the world held its breath.

Somewhere else, somewhere warm and breezy where the air smelled like suntan lotion and sand, a father paused from folding shirts into a suitcase he would carry on a plane the next morning and padded into the family room so he could circle his arms around his husband, rest his chin on the taller man's shoulder, and deliver assurances into his ear.

It will be all right.

It will be better than okay.

It will be amazing.

Near a trailer home parked just outside of a Nowhere Town, a girl who had sought stardom elsewhere but had to return home to find it sat on a rock with a view of the foggy South

Carolina woods. If her fans had seen her in that lonely moment, they might have assumed she was praying, seeking a divine spirit to guide her in the taxing work of guiding souls on Earth. With her head tilted back to the sky, pressed palms raised to her pressed lips, she was indeed praying—just not to the heavens. She was praying to her strength, to whatever resources she had within, to help her walk away. The cost she was paying for fame was too great, and she had so much living left to do.

Somewhere, a woman in a sequined dress as tight as her own skin and heels so tall they made her feel like a supermodel warrior delivered a punch line in a candle-lit cabaret. Even as laughter rolled toward her from an audience she could not see, even with the heat of the stage lights pressing down on her like that of a lassoed sun, she didn't blink. She didn't falter.

Somewhere, two dreamers made the most of their failed utopia, while a single mother held her sleeping baby to her chest and whispered promises into his ear. "I will love you always. I will always be here." At the same time, a rock star pulled the brim of his hat down low, slid dark sunglasses on his face, and stepped off an airplane in a city two hours from the place he had worked so hard to escape but was now choosing to return to.

Somewhere, a guy who had never been anywhere before told a group of physicists about the time he sang in the shower and then learned how to dance, and a thirteen-year-old prodigy forgot that he was a genius because he was at a party standing next to his new best friend and a girl he hadn't met yet was smiling at him from across the room.

Somewhere, in a barn in a field north of everywhere else, a scientist—who was neither a wizard nor a god, just a person who wanted to save the world—waited for the clock above his desk to chime. And when it did, another scientist in a deserted corner of a vast continent flipped a switch.

It

    Was

        Spectacular.

ACKNOWLEDGMENTS

This story would not have become exactly what it is without Second Book Syndrome, self-help podcasts, Rumi's poetry, too much time alone, NPR, Mark Twain's *Adventures of Huckleberry Finn*, Jack Kerouac, self-doubt, John Bunyan's *The Pilgrim's Progress*, a suitcase filled with mixed tapes, a Jeep Cherokee named "Little Tank," *The Canterbury Tales*, *Don Quixote*, *The Wonderful Wizard of Oz*, Homer's *The Odyssey*, John Steinbeck's *Travels with Charley*, Bill Bryson, Neil deGrasse Tyson, astrophysics, theology, the University of Cambridge's Centre for the Study of Existential Risk, *One Hundred Years of Solitude*, *Siddhartha*, National Geographic coffee-table photography books, three-a.m. insomnia, a defective GPS, the original Dr. Az (Abd al-Rahman al-Sufi), a cross-country train ride with a long layover in the Mojave Desert, Henry James, Ralph Waldo Emerson, Maria Mitchell, a fantastic road trip that included the length of Oklahoma and the worst Thai food I will ever eat, heartbreak, luck, delayed planes, Greek mythology, people who use religion to justify atrocities as well as believers whose convictions offer a giving and healing light, existential angst, absolute love, and the realization that faith manifests itself in so very many forms.

Thank you to my agent, Stephen Barbara, who coaches me through the spots where I can't tell my left from my right and does so graciously.

Thank you, Sarah Dotts Barley, my editor for *Even in Paradise*, for giving my first novel a home and believing in me so much. I'm still amazed that Erica Sussman, an editor as diligent as she is thoughtful, wanted to work with me. *Be Good Be Real Be Crazy* is an exponentially better book because of her.

If I could melt my gratitude to liquid form, it would flood the offices of the many HarperCollins folks who helped usher *BGBRBC* into the universe. Thank you, Renée Cafiero, Alison Donalty, Erin Fitzsimmons, Stephanie Hoover, Joey Jachowski, Jenna Stempel, and Elizabeth Ward.

I am grateful to have access to smart people who know what I don't and have experienced what I have not. Thank you to Coleman Barks for giving me permission to quote his translations of Rumi's poetry. Thank you, Laura and Brian Rossbert, for helping me untangle physics and theology and then jumble them back up again. Thank you to Chuda Niroula and his family. I was only a friend of a friend, and yet you opened your home and shared your stories about day-to-day existence in refugee camps and what it means to leave a place forever behind. Thank you to Eamon Aghdasi for correcting my Farsi and to every librarian who, over the past two years, has turned me in the right direction.

My "kidney friends," please know that I am amazed to have you in my life. I am blessed by your support. If you asked me to, I'd swim to Pluto and back. I'd catch the feeling of a summer evening in a jar and discover new constellations to name after each of you. I'd attempt so many impossible things because you deserve nothing less than incredible.

Thank you to my family (my parents, Karen and Bill Philpot, and my siblings, Natalie, Saeger, and Harris) for being my gravity. Thank you with sprinkles on top to my little sister, Saeger, and my brother-in-law Chris for giving me space and time to think and write. I am inspired by the depth of your generosity and the strength of your accepting hearts.

Levi, I met you and the universe did pause. You are extraordinary. If I haven't made that clear already, then over the years I will. Promise.

I have lived three lifetimes in the past two years. At the most confusing parts, I've felt like my orbit was off. That I was spinning too fast and getting stuck in corners that shouldn't exist. However, time and time again, readers pulled me back to earth by reminding me why I love what I do.

Dear readers, please know that I am honored and awed by

you. If something in my words spoke to you, I'm glad. If you've made me think about my own work in a new way, I'm thankful. So, so thankful.

This all, this everything, is, indeed, spectacular.

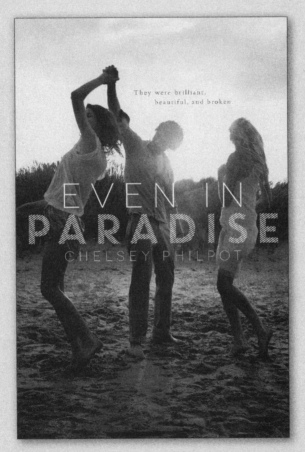